About the author

The author has had an undying interest in naval warfare and the Royal Navy in particular from a very early age. He is also, a very keen ship modeller, with many models winning awards. He has written in many modelling magazines over the years, on various warship articles. He served thirty-five years in the civil aviation field and fifteen years patrolling the motorways. Now retired, he has the time to turn to his first love, the Royal Navy.

IN OUR DARKEST HOUR

Ron Wilkinson

IN OUR DARKEST HOUR

Vanguard Press

VANGUARD PAPERBACK

© Copyright 2021
Ron Wilkinson

The right of Ron Wilkinson to be identified as author of this work has been asserted by him in accordance with the Copyright, Designs and Patents Act 1988.

All Rights Reserved

No reproduction, copy or transmission of this publication may be made without written permission.
No paragraph of this publication may be reproduced, copied or transmitted save with the written permission of the publisher, or in accordance with the provisions of the Copyright Act 1956 (as amended).

Any person who commits any unauthorised act in relation to this publication may be liable to criminal prosecution and civil claims for damages.

A CIP catalogue record for this title is available from the British Library.

ISBN 978-1-80016-101-6

*Vanguard Press is an imprint of
Pegasus Elliot MacKenzie Publishers Ltd.*
www.pegasuspublishers.com

First Published in 2021

**Vanguard Press
Sheraton House Castle Park
Cambridge England**

Printed & Bound in Great Britain

Dedication

To Carol, David, Natalie, Jessica and Sam. Love you all.

Acknowledgements

To all at Pegasus Elliot MacKenzie Publishers: grateful thanks.

She emerged from the mist, two smoky tugs fussing about her, her shape distorted and smoke blackened. The noise from her pumps making a regular sound as they kept the sea out of her battered hull. Her bedraggled ensign hanging limply from her main mast. H.M.S. *Preston* was finally home. As the tugs pushed and cajoled her against the dock wall, the dockyard mateys looked up at her battered side and shook their heads. It was going to be a long time before 'Proud' *Preston* was back in the war.

On the bridge, the captain, Commander Alan Lee R.N. DSO MiD, looked around, seeing the excited faces of sailors eager to go on leave.

"Ring off main engines, No. 1" he said in a quiet voice, "and make sure the watch is ready for leave. As soon as I see the Admiral, I can get an update on repairs, and make sure the damage list is up to date"

"Aye, aye, Skipper. I have just seen the Engineer, so the list is correct," replied Lt Cdr Alf Matley R.N.

"Thanks, No. 1."

There was a flurry on the dockside as a RN Staff car pulled up at the gangway. Fortunately the gangway sentry was in place just in time, and the Officer of the Day was present. The bridge telephone rang.

"Captain?"

"Yes Guns."

"Dock Admiral is here to see you, sir!" reported OOD Lt Beddall RN, the Gunnery Officer.

"OK, on my way down. No. 1, brass coming aboard. Damn, I wanted a bath, shave, and a clean uniform, before seeing him!"

"Very good sir I will tell your steward, it could be good news!" Alf smiled.

"Ha I don't think so, thanks, No. 1."

Making his way aft, avoiding the damaged areas and sailors going about their duties, the familiar faces, looked questionably at him as he passed, "Leave, sir?" the face of a Leading Hand, still with his head bandaged, asks, "I hope so Hooky. Look lively, Brass Hat coming aboard!"

"Aye, aye."

On the quarterdeck, somehow the OOD (Officer of the Day) had organised a smart side party — thank god for Beddall! With a twitter of 'Bosuns calls' the Admiral and his staff, were piped aboard.

Saluting and stepping forward to meet Admiral John Tremaine RN, Lee shook hands. The Admiral and his staff all looked immaculate and shiny compared to him and his crew.

"Sorry to spring this on you, Alan, but we need to have chat before you give leave! Please stand your men down, and ask your Engineer and No. 1, to join us."

"Yes sir" nodding to the OOD who had the tannoy already in his hands. "Please come aft to my day cabin, sir."

Leading the way across the smashed quarterdeck and down the deck hatch, they crossed the lobby and into the rarely used day cabin, where Timmins, his steward had arranged a few nibbles and coffee for the guests. With a smile and a nod he left the cabin. Another of *Proud Preston's* excellent crew members. Looking at the spread, the Admiral said, "If you want to get rid of your steward Alan, I will take him!" he laughed.

"I don't think that will happen, sir! Please everybody, help yourselves to coffee or spirits, smoke if you wish."

Arranged around the captain's table, squeezed in the Admiral, Flag Lieutenant, Alan, No. 1, the Engineer, Dockyard Superintendent and a couple of other people, all clutching notepads.

"So, we have had to change our plans for your refit, Alan. We plan to send you to New York, we don't have the capacity to repair you here in the UK. The Fleet took a battering in the evacuation from Crete, so there are no dockyards available."

"I see, sir. What about leave for my men?"

"Right, the dockyard will do what repairs are needed here to make you seaworthy. We will lift 'A' turret out to take off some of the strain from the forward bulkheads. This will take about fourteen days, so leave can be given for each watch for seven days."

"Right sir, I was hoping for a bit longer we have not been home for a long time."

"Can't be helped Alan, they should get a rest in the US."

The next few hours were taken up with discussion on detailed repairs and a myriad of other issues. Lee was desperately tired, and just wanted to retire to his bunk and sleep the sleep of the just. Finally, as the visitors all left, Lee and his No 1 sat with a glass of gin at the table and discussed what was going to happen over the next few weeks.

Chapter 1

It's late spring 1939 and Commander Alan Lee stands on the dockside at Swan Hunters' Ship Builders, looking up at his new command. Resplendent in her Far East fleet colours of gleaming white hull and superstructure, with buff coloured funnels and mast's. HMS *Preston* is ready for her departure to Hong Kong. Lee is taking over from her previous Captain who has been admitted to hospital with a mysterious illness, requiring his removal from command.

Preston is the last of the Town class cruisers built for the Royal Navy, at 10,000 tons displacement and a length of 591feet, armed with twelve, six-inch guns in four turrets, eight, four-inch guns in four turrets, eight torpedo tubes, two Walrus aircraft and light anti-aircraft guns. She represents the best in Royal Navy cruisers — fast, well-armed and handsome ships. Built in response to the powerful *Mogami* class cruisers of the Japanese navy.

He wonders what the future will bring, war with Germany looks imminent. After the 'War to end all Wars' how could we slide down this slope again? However, that is for the future, now it was off to foreign lands to 'Show the Flag'.

Shakedown took eight days, and the few minor faults rectified, now completed, Alan accepts the ship on behalf of the Admiralty. He is presented with a silver salver as a memento of this occasion.

Preston proceeds down the North Sea, into the Channel, weaving through the various ferries and coasters going about their business. Lee works on getting the ship's company up to speed, especially the new officers. On down the English Channel, all navigation lights blazing, and searchlights pointing to the sky, this was His Majesties latest warship going about her business, then into Plymouth for fuel. It would appear that a lot of Plymouth residents had turned out to see the latest warship for the King's Fleet. The Hoe and Barbican were packed with happy people. As a student of naval history, he glanced across at Jennycliff Beach, and in his mind's eye, he could see the old 'Line of Battleship' *HMS Bellerophon*, anchored there. A crowd of sightseeing boats clustered all around her, desperately looking for a sight of Napoleon, the only time he came to Britain.

As his ship turned in the Sound, Lee watched the construction taking place at Mount Batten, where a new seaplane base was being constructed. Would that be needed in the future? We shall see.

Refuelled, and the latest orders taken onboard. The following day they departed from Plymouth, next stop Gibraltar, followed by Malta, Aden, Colombo,

Singapore and finally Hong Kong. It was like a Thomas Cook Tour itinerary.

Born at the turn of the century, Alan Lee entered the Navy at the age of fourteen. The son of a minor official in the Admiralty, his parents insisted on his attendance at Britannia, the Royal Naval College at Dartmouth, where he passed out second in his term. Life was hard, his parents had little spare money to help him through his schooling, but somehow, he managed to survive.

From *Britannia*, he went to join the brand-new cruiser *Caroline*, attached to the Grand Fleet, based at Scapa Flow. He spent a happy two years onboard, where he was promoted to Sub-Lieutenant, specialising in navigation. *Caroline* was present at the Battle of Jutland, where she acquitted herself well. In 1917, after promotion to Lieutenant, he was transferred to the Tribal class destroyer *Mohawk*. She was stationed at Dover, patrolling the Dover Barrage. This was the line of nets and minefields, that stretched from the English to the French coast. This provided protection to the Dover Straits from marauding German U-boats and destroyers, these both being based at Zeebrugge and Bruges. The swift action, and cut and trust of this type of warfare really suited the young Lieutenant.

On St George's Day, 1918, *Mohawk* took part in the raid on Zeebrugge, where Lee was slightly wounded, and was awarded a Mention in Dispatches for his calmness under fire. After the war, he joined a few ships and did two spells of service at the Admiralty Building, which he hated. Steady promotion was the order of the day, until he joined *Preston*.

Now he was cruising the exotic Far East with *Preston*, received many foreign visitors, who came aboard to admire the ship. Cocktail parties were common along with large mess bills for the officers, and many women in low-cut dresses came aboard to tease the young sailors. The 'Fishing Fleet' is in full flow! (The Fishing Fleet was a slang term used to describe the daughters of Government officials who were based abroad, who desperately wanted to unburden themselves of expensive daughters onto prospective husbands aboard HM Ships).

Preston was ordered to the Sea of Japan, to watched the Japanese fleet manoeuvres. She was a very unwelcome guest! Later berthed in Kobe Harbour, Lee was very impressed by the attitude of the Japanese sailors; they would make a formidable enemy.

During this time, he had also been monitoring the signals from the Admiralty, and it was becoming very clear that the political situation was deteriorating and that there would soon be conflict.

After spending a few happy months of peacetime cruising, now with war being declared, her gleaming paint now had been replaced with 'pusser grey', all brightwork dulled down and the holystoned decks allowed to fade to a grey colour.

Preston commenced to escort convoys in the Indian Ocean. Next, escorting the first ANZAC convoy to Egypt. Then searching for Blockade Runners and the surface raider, the pocket battleship *Graf Spee*.

After four months, she was recalled to the UK. She left Singapore, and a quick call at Trincomalee for fuel, then into that furnace, called Aden, where she refuelled and awaited orders. After five days she received orders to transit the Suez Canal calling at Alexandra for fuel and mail.

Leaving Aden with a wonderful sea breeze caressing the ship, she headed north. Having been a Midshipman in WWI, Lee was very aware of the need for vigilance and practice drills. So, he trained the ship's company hard — damage control, fire, boat handling, towing, launching and recovery of aircraft, but most of all gunnery! He was blessed in his Gunnery Officer Mark Beddall, as a regular, he had specialised in gunnery and had passed out at Whale Island top of his term. Always looking to improve the efficiency of his department, he drilled his men remorseless. In the fleet cruise to Wei Hei Wei, China, *Preston* outshot all competitors and won the 'Cock of the Fleet' gunnery award. Having been presented with the award by the Admiral of the Far East Fleet, Lee was chastised for wearing out the gun barrels, which need relining. Obviously, the Admiral didn't know about the sticking turret ring on 'X' gun mount.

From Alexandria to Gibraltar, *Preston* switched to a defence state as the shooting war came closer. Berthing at the Detached Mole in Gibraltar, Lee is summoned to HQ deep inside the Gibraltar tunnels. New orders?

"No. 1, have the boat crew take me ashore, and give each watch six hours leave to take in the sights of Gib and get a few trinkets to take home. Also, ask the engineer to contact the dockyard for the spare parts he needs, and finish the refuelling, thanks."

Entering the dark, dank tunnels at HQ Gibraltar, Lee was struck by the frenetic activity, as staff moved around the place, all appearing to be clutching pieces of paper! The Admiral commanding Gibraltar, barely looked up from his desk.

"Fresh orders, Captain, speak to my Flag Lieutenant if you need anything," and with a nod he was dismissed.

Ushered into a side office, he was confronted by a harassed assistant. "Your orders Sir, sail in the morning at 0700 sharp to make the rendezvous!"

Rendezvous? What was that about? His mind was working overtime as he made his way back to the ship.

Safely back aboard, Lee retired to his day cabin, where lunch was ready, and opened his orders.

'In all respects ready for sea. HMS *Preston* is to proceed to an area north-west of Cape Verde Island, where you are to await and intercept the blockade runner *Bremen,* which is en-route for Hamburg in

Germany with a load of rubber and precious metals, to capture if possible or to sink her.' He reached for the telephone to the Wardroom, "No 1, Guns and Navigator to the Captain's Day cabin!"

A few moments later a knock at his cabin door, and in came the three officers.

"Sit down gents, help yourselves to the gin."

Spread across the table was a navigation map for the area around Cape Verde. "Gents, these are our orders. Pilot, I need a course and ETA to the area for arrival in two days, as economical a speed as possible!"

"Sir."

"No. 1, how are we with refuelling, spares and victualing?"

No. 1, Lt Cdr. Gil Nunn RN, replied, "Fuelling will be completed by 2100, victuals are aboard, but the dockyard was unable to help with spares. Leave is up at 2200, so we will be able to sail on time."

"Good, thanks. Guns, everything squared away with your department?"

"Yes, sir, only the barrel wear and the turret ring on 'X' turret sticking, but we will need Guzz to sort that out."

"Very good, I don't know where their Lordships get their information from but if it's true this will be a blow to the Third Reich! Get some rest gents, we sail at 0700, that's all."

0645, "Special sea duty men close up! Hands for leaving harbour" squawks the tannoy, "Defence stations close up." Muttering and grumbling, the hands head to their stations, a normal reaction, but if Jack wasn't moaning, it was not a good day! 'If you can't take a joke, you shouldn't have joined!', how often had that been heard?

On the bridge, all was quiet, a gentle hum from the engine room fans, and the whispered conversation amongst the signalmen.

"Ship closed up, coxswain on the wheel, postman aboard, ready to leave harbour sir!"

"Thanks, No. 1, let go forward and aft, slow ahead, port five degrees."

Preston headed for the boom at the south entrance to the harbour, the light weapons sniffing the air for any threat to the ship. A destroyer in the trots blinks a message, 'Good Hunting'. "Acknowledge 'Thanks'," said Lee.

Outside the harbour, *Preston* increased speed and headed for the Straits. Unwanted eyes watched as *Preston* headed towards the Cape Verde Islands. A radio message is sent to the German Naval Intelligence, the *Abwehr*, "British Town class Cruiser, leaving Gibraltar, heading Atlantic." Into a rising sea, *Preston* shouldered her way forward.

"OOW, ask the 'Fly boys' to come to the Bridge," instructed Lee.

The two aircraft crews stood before him, "Gentlemen, I want to start a dawn patrol out to 200 miles to the north and north-west, please can you organize a plan, and let me know? OOW, stand the crew down, set security state three and send the hands to breakfast."

In the engine room, Lt Cdr. Eric Jones RN stood on the control panel grating, the roar of fans and machinery defended any sound and amongst his gleaming instruments and gauges, he was king of all he surveys. Old for his rank, he was as content as a man at the pinnacle of his career, starting as a boy stoker, he had worked his way to the top, and now commanded the machinery of one of the Royal Navy's premier warships. Having been with the ship from keel laying, he knew every inch of her spaces, and was proud of her machinery. Capable of 32 knots on trials, he knew he could get more out of her, but not at the moment, that damn port recycling pump was still playing up. Unable to get spares at Trinco or Gib he had to keep an eye on it; hence he had one of his stokers watching it. Now in the Atlantic the temperature had fallen in the engineering spaces to a more acceptable level, after Aden where his men could only manage thirty minutes at a time in the heat, thank goodness that was over. Moving over to the faulty pump, and using sign language, he checked on his stoker. With a thumbs up and a smile, he knew at the moment all is well. Whistling a silent tune, he continued his inspection of the boiler and engine rooms.

"Ten minutes to sun up sir, hands at action stations and both aircraft ready to launch." Speaking quietly,

Nunn, the executive officer, or No. 1 to everybody, saluted the captain.

"Thanks, No. 1, turn the *Preston* to starboard 30 degrees to launch the first aircraft."

Needing a bit more lift, it was easier to turn the ship, to give more wind for the Walrus to take off. The signalman dropped his flag and with a loud bang and a whoosh, the Walrus staggered into the air.

"Twenty minutes to ready the other aircraft and launch, sir."

"Very Good."

The acrid smell of cordite drifted over the bridge as Lee watched the aircraft slowly climb away, and pondered how an aircraft designer could design such an ugly duckling as the Walrus, and the beautiful Spitfire. Still glad the country had both.

Preston carried four midshipmen, officers under training, so during the quiet times they could be given jobs to do, to increase their knowledge. The Chief Yeoman came forward to the Captain, "Message from the Admiralty, sir. Top Secret."
Nodding, he took the message from the signalman and passed it to Midshipman Devonshire, "Take this to the coding office, Mr Devonshire and have it decoded and be quick! Mr. Vickers, I need to see your journal, bring it to the bridge please."

"Sir," as the terrified midshipman ran from the bridge.

"Walk, Mr Vickers," smiles all round.

"Ah! we were all young once," said Guns.

Another bang and the second Walrus lurched into the air, and heads of in a different direction.

"Pilot, return to our course."

Lee retired to his sea cabin, for a bath, something to eat and the endless paperwork — lists for everything, promotions, warrants it never stops. Fortunately, the Paymaster handled most of it, but he still needed to check and sign everything. Sometime later, as he picked up his coffee cup, the phone rang, "Captain here."

"Bridge here, Captain. First Walrus returning, nothing to report."

"Very good, I will come up!"

Moments later standing on the gratings, binoculars to his eyes, he watched the 'shagbat' make its sedately way back to the ship. Closer to the ship, he ordered, "Hands to recover aircraft. OOW turn the *Preston* 30 degrees to port." This was to leave a slick of smooth water behind the ship to help give the aircraft a safe landing.

The aircraft slowed down and caressed the water slick, but bounced up a few feet, before settling onto the water. The Observer climbed onto the upper wing, ready to collect the crane hook, just a few feet from the turning propeller. The aircraft came alongside and the crane swung out and lowered the hook for the aircraft. Out of the water, the aircraft swung precariously close to the ship's side, steadying ropes and poles corral the aircraft, and it's landed onto the aircraft trolly.

Over the horizon, the second aircraft appeared, its Aldis lamp flashing furiously. "Suspect merchant ship 150 miles south west 200 degrees," a yeoman reads the message.

"No. 1, get the aircraft aboard as quick as you can and get the Pilot to plot a course," Lee's mind was working out his plan of action.

The Walrus approached the ship, and again *Preston* turned to port to help the landing. The aircraft slowed down and touched the water, then started to porpoise just as a wave rose up to strike the underside, ripping the starboard float off, and pitching the aircraft over onto its back. Many things happened at once.

"Ship hard a port."

"Away boats crew."

"Lower scrambling nets."

The crew looked on with horror on their faces. The Walrus was now nose down with just the tail plane above water. It took about fifteen minutes for the seaboat to be launched and make to the rapidly disappearing aircraft. The boat's coxswain bravely dived into the sea to try to help. After trying a few times, he was unsuccessful, and the aircraft disappeared into the blackness.

"Recall the seaboat, OOW," Lee commanded. Looking around the bridge, he was struck by the look of shock on the crew's faces, the loss of any crew mates was always hard especially after being together for so long.

"Ask the seaboat coxswain to report to the bridge and Boatswain, give the seaboat crew a tot of rum."

"Sir."

"OOW, make a note in the log and mark the spot on the charts, the relatives will like to know where their loved ones lie."

A bedraggled looking Leading Seaman, Steve De Asha, arrived on the bridge.

"You wanted me, sir?"

"Yes, just to thank you for your efforts just now, please join the boat crew with the Buffer for an extra tot!"

"Aye, aye, sir, thanks."

"Set course for that merchant ship and prepare the aircraft for another flight. Bring the ship up to 25 knots, please."

Settling on her new course and speed, *Preston* shivered as if to shake off the memory of the past hour. Back to normal routine.

Later, "Aircraft signalling. Ship heading is due north, speed 12 knots, ignoring our signals," reports the signal man.

"Very good. Action stations, No. 1, seaboat's crew and boarding party to assemble in the port waist!"

Alarm rattlers sound through the ship, men move around in a purposeful manner.

"Battle Bowlers, everyone," the captain commanded.

"Ship closed up at action stations sir, all Boilers on line." No. 1 passed the message, then left for his action station at the rear conning position.

"Very good. Bridge... DCT anything in sight, Guns?"

"DCT... Bridge, smoke directly ahead."

"Pilot, well done, right on the bow."

The Navigator Lt Smyth, embarrassed, muttered, "Thank you, sir."

"DCT... Bridge, we are closing right astern, I don't think they have seen us, she's slowing!"

Still invisible from the bridge, Lee watched the sun, "What time's sunset, Nav?"

"Two hours. Sir. 1900."

"Shagbat signalling, submarine alongside the ship! Attacking!"

"No! Tell her to stand off," screamed Lee.

A bright flash on the horizon signalled something had happened, but what? DCT couldn't make out anything at this distance.

"Chief Yeoman, raise the airplane. Mr Vickers, make a note in the action log, get the position from Mr Smyth, but do not transmit to the Admiralty until I say so."

"Aye, aye."

"No reply from the aircraft, sir."

"OK, keep trying."

Lee was thinking out loud: What has happened, oh, how I wish for one of those new-fangled radar sets. But others had priority on them.

Smyth replied, "I was on board *Manchester* at Gib, they were saying it's fantastic. They can 'see' up to fifty miles away. Maybe one day!"

Lee grunted. "DCT... Bridge, ship is hull up sir, can't see the Walrus. She's spotted us, and increased speed, sir."

Lee could see the plume of smoke rising from the merchantman's spindly funnel, "DCT, any sign of the sub?"

"No, sir, only the merchant ship in sight."

Damn, where was that sub? Picking up the phone, he contacted the aft steering position. "No. 1, I want your opinion on this." And explained the scenario. Nunn was an ex-submariner, so his insight was useful.

"Sir, if I have torpedoes left, I would lie in wait to tinfish us!"

"Yes, my thoughts as well. Thanks, No. 1. OK, Port 25, bring her up to 28 knots, start zig zag, asdic start transmitting, and signal that ship to heave to!" ordered Lee.

"No response from the enemy, sir," Bunts calls

So, it's the enemy now, how things have changed!

"OK Guns, put a shell across her bows, let's see if that gets her attention."

Watching 'B' gun turn slightly on its roller path and the barrels raise into the air, then it settled on its bearing.

'Ting, ting' went the firing bell, 'bang' and the bridge was swept by the shockwave and the smell of cordite. Moments later, a flume of seawater rose beyond the bows of the merchant ship.

"DCT... Bridge, confirm the ship is *Bremen* sir! We can see her name on the stern."

So, it was the *Bremen*, no doubt now. How did the Admiralty know? Still, that was a question for another day, where was that damn sub? Lee brain was working overtime.

"Any response from the *Bremen*, Bunts?"

"No, sir, still silence."

"OK, tell him if he does not heave too, I will sink his ship and leave the crew in the boats!"

"OK, sir." Clack clack clack went the shutter on the signal lamp. Where was that sub?

From the bridge repeater, he could hear the satisfying ping from the asdic set. Probably too far away to be any use, but as a deterrent weapon it helped. He looked around to check the lookouts were scanning their areas of responsibility; glad they were not watching the *Bremen*.

"No reply from the enemy ship, sir."

"OK thanks. Guns, one more round across her bows."

Bang! Closer this time, and the familiar water spout. "Guns load HE rounds and await my orders, looks like we will have to sink her, I will manoeuvre to keep us bows on."

"Sir."

"Periscope! Red 45 8,000 yards!" shouted the port lookout, "Torpedoes in the water heading straight for us!"

Lee flew across the bridge, "Hard a starboard, port engine full astern, starboard engine full ahead!" *Preston* turned sluggishly, Lee watched with fascination as the two torpedoes headed straight towards his ship! Come on, come on turn, he banged his hand on the bridge screen, as *Preston* turned slowly. The first torpedo slammed into the stern of the ship, 'clang' and a plume of water rose above the quarterdeck, dirty brown water cascading onto the wooden decks. The second torpedo missed astern by feet.

"Chief Yeoman, message to Admiralty repeated VA Gibraltar am under attack from submarine, get our position from the Pilot."

"Aye, sir."

"Damage control, I need a report. Engine Room report damage, helm a midships, let's stay on this heading for a while," said Lee. The reports started to filter onto the bridge, unbelievably the torpedo hadn't detonated, but *Preston* was holed aft in the port wing compartment, and minor shock damage in adjoining areas. How lucky had 'Proud' *Preston* been! Minor damage in the engine room, but nothing serious.

"Warship bearing green 25," reported the lookout, the DCT trained round on the new bearing, enemy or friends? It never rains!

"Two warships bearing green 25," sang out a second lookout. Two V and W destroyers headed towards *Preston*, "Can we be of assistance," flashed *Wild Swan*.

"Pass the position of that sub and ask them to take a look, while we stop the leak down aft."

Jones, the Engineer, stood by Lee's bridge chair, "Not bad aft sir, it could have been a lot worse, the pumps have lowered the water and the hole has been packed. I can still give you full speed and the damage would take a dockyard about a week to fix."

"Thanks, Eric, tell your team well done."

Lee turned to watch as the two destroyers sped past. Built to fight in the last war, they now served in this, with their short fat funnel aft and a tall thin funnel forward, they looked anarchic. But they could still be deadly to submarine or surface ship. *Vimy* headed toward the *Bremen*, "Ask *Vimy* to deal with the sub first, *Bremen* can wait."

"*Wild Swan* is attacking," shouted the lookout, "Cor, look at her go."

"Silence!" shouted the CPO.

Ten huge water spouts rose out of the sea as *Wild Swan* plastered the sub with depth charges. *Vimy* changed course to attack, giving *Wild Swan* time to leave the area. *Vimy* ran in, again ten large waterspouts rose from the sea. This pattern was repeated for the next thirty minutes, as the destroyers took it in turns to attack.

Unknown to the destroyers, the submarine U-97 was dying, all lights had gone out, and emergency red lights were on. Various leaks were entering the boat, and the smell of battery acid was strong. The boat would not answer the helm and the HP air had escaped, so she would not rise.

U-boat Captain, Müller, awaited his fate. What idiot ordered us to meet up with *Bremen*? Why didn't the torpedo explode? Things he would never know the answers to.

Looking around the control room at his men, they were all terrified, he tried to make them relax, but it was not working. He thought about his brother, Hans, a pilot on a Bomber Geschwader stationed in France. He would have liked to have seen him again, and go exploring the forests near their parents' home. The last letter from him was full of confidence, and bashing the Tommies!

With a loud woosh his command imploded, taking all aboard to a cold deep grave.

"Bridge, breaking up noises," the asdic office reports over the tannoy. Cheering erupted from the bridge staff, everybody with a smile on their faces!

"Well done, *Wild Swan* and *Vimy*, splice the main brace," signalled *Preston*.

"Sir, the *Bremen* is sinking," reported the lookout. Damn, thought Lee, I wanted that ship captured.

"OK, ask *Vimy* to pick up survivors."

Later a message from *Wild Swan*. It read, "I believe I have something that belongs to you? Three very wet airmen!"

More cheering on the bridge, thank god for that, at least that aircraft crew are safe!

"Signal, when you have dried them out and at your pleasure can you return them. OOW, ask the chef to bake some fresh bread — the *Wild Swan* will want a reward! And stand down action station and set defence watch 3. Pilot course for home and reduce speed to 20 knots."

At a steady course and speed, *Wild Swan* eased alongside *Preston* to do a jackstay transfer. The three airmen were coming home. Usually the game was to try and get the legs of the jackstay transferee wet, but not this time, the three men landed on *Preston* deck all safe and sound and dry, after all they are *Prestonians*!

Later *Vimy* came alongside to transfer the eighty-three survivors, there was not enough room onboard the destroyer to house so many enemies safely. With no aircraft now embarked they were put in one of the empty aircraft hangars and a Royal Marine guard instigated. CPO Carrie, the Chief Telegraphist, came to Lee, "Sir, I was wondering, I have two German speaking 'Tels' onboard, if you wanted, I could get them to 'listen in' on their conversations, we might find something out?"

"Good idea, CPO, see to it, and thanks."

Home, it had been a long twelve months since the *Preston* had left for the Far East, so much had changed.

Sat in his bridge chair, Lee watched as *Preston* approached the Plymouth Breakwater, smoke and dust hung over the dockyard, a legacy of last night's bomber raid. Looking to the right, Lee can see some families on Bovisands Beach, waving, somebody must have a relative in the dockyard, so much for security. The ship's engineers and the Buffer had made good some of the damage, but the signal in his hand stated that *Preston* was having a full refit, so all the damage would be made good. Two tugs waited behind the boom to assist in docking *Preston*. The harbour pilot was aboard one of the tugs, much to Smyth's annoyance, as he wanted to pilot the ship in to the dockyard. However, better to be safe than sorry, after all there will be many 'Brass Hats' watching.

"No. 1, man the sides, but leave the defence watch closed up, we don't want any nasty surprises."

The harbour pilot came aboard. "Pilot, you have the ship," Lee spoke to the bridge.

Wild Swan and *Vimy* followed *Preston*, then headed for the Duty Oiler, destroyers got little rest. "Bunts, message to *Wild Swan* repeated *Vimy*, Captain and Executive Officers repair on board at 1800. No.1 with your permission, a social evening in the wardroom for the destroyers?" It was protocol that the Captain had to ask the executive officer for permission to enter the wardroom. Lee was very happy to reverse roles.

"My thought exactly sir! I will contact the wardroom steward," No. 1 smiled.

Through the Sound and around Drake's Island, passing Devil's Point to starboard, its razor-sharp rocks waiting to grab any unwary passing ship, through the inner boom and into the Hamoaze, *Preston* headed for her berth. As the ship was eased against the jetty wall at the Devonport's south yard, Lee watched the activity as the ship was tied to the bollards, gangways passed, and an Army armed guard stood by for the prisoners. Thinking to himself, pity we didn't learn anything from the prisoners, maybe the Army will do better.

Then the inevitable visitations of many people to start the process of the refit. Knowing the refit would take twenty weeks, he ordered three weeks' leave for each watch, but before that the ammunition lighter was pushed alongside to de-ammunition the ship. Going on leave, the crew would undoubtedly be quick with the offload.

Chapter 2

Lee stood on the bridge gratings, returned from leave he was rested and refreshed. Living in Eggbuckland, he had been able to get home every evening during the refit, apart from two weeks in Dover. His family fully appreciated the visits. Looking around his command, red lead paint was everywhere, welding gear, clatter of riveting guns, cables, wires, tools underfoot, what a mess. He made his way aft to his day cabin and the inevitable pile of paperwork! While they were in dock, the Navy had not been resting. The campaign in Norway for the Navy, had at first gone well, but then the loss of an aircraft carrier, cruiser and destroyers had left a bitter taste.

Dunkirk, the destroyers and other smaller warships had taken a beating, but they had done the job and the 'Pongos were home! Lee had listened on the radio at the growing numbers of returned soldiers, everyday wishing it to be over. He contacted the Admiralty to see if he could help. But they said it was under control so enjoy your leave. The very next day, Lee received an urgent call from the Admiralty. He was to make his way with all dispatch, and report to Admiral Bertram Ramsey in Dover Castle. There he spent two weeks, assisting in the planning of the evacuation, going across to Dunkirk and Calais on a couple of occasions to get more information on what was needed. There he received his baptism of fire to air attacks, and the nerve-jangling scream from the 'Jericho Trumpets' fitted to the diving Ju 87 Stuka dive-bombers.

The ship had changed, the new radar lantern now sat atop the bridge, its all-seeing eye ready for action, workmen still working on it. He had been on a course to see it in action and was impressed, let's hope it lives up to the hype! Six new 20mm Oerlikon cannons sat in tubs around the ship, replacing those useless 0.5in machine guns. The single two pdrs, now exchanged for four-barrel Pom-poms, a vast improvement to the defence of the ship. Extra armour had been worked into the ship, the action damage had been made good. Other changes, large and small, had taken place, but this also meant an increase in the number of crew. It had been decided that in future the ship would only carry one Walrus, this meant that the spare aircraft hangar, could be converted into more messes and offices, a useful addition.

The crew had also changed. He had lost two hundred seasoned sailors of all ranks, for promotions, training, to man new construction, and to feed the hungry need of a growing fleet. Their replacements were Hostility Only ratings, straight from the Training Depots, they would need watching, especially as many had never been to sea before. He also lost Nunn his trusty second in command, promoted to the Captain of one of those Corvettes *HMS Pimpernel*. He was sorry to see him go, but knew that he would do well. Luckily, he had retained Guns and the Chief, but also lost the Navigator, he had gone to join one of the new aircraft carriers being built. His new Executive Officer Lt Cdr. Alf Matley RN had come straight from one of the destroyers sunk at Narvik, and after survivor's leave was here. The Navigator had not arrived yet. Finally, he had lost two Midshipmen and gained two more, we will see how they shape up.

Two weeks later *Preston* was ready for sea. The dockyard had worked miracles, smart and tidy, and resplendent in her new two-tone grey paint. As a thank you, to the dockyard mateys, they had hosted a party for their children, which had gone down well. Now she was again a man of war. Ready for her shakedown. Lee called a conference in his cabin.

"The ship being in aspects ready for sea, you are to proceed to Scapa Flow." So started his orders. Scapa, those wind-swept islands off the North Scottish coast, home of the Home Fleet. "Where you will commence work-up ready for deployment to the Mediterranean." So that's the plan from their Lordships for *Preston*.

He looked around the heads of departments and CPOs. "Are you all happy your departments are on top line, with no snags?" Confirmation all round. "We have a lot of baby sailors onboard so I want the training to start straight away, so we will have a good idea of what we have by the time we reach Scapa, understood?" said Lee

Looking around his cabin, all the heads nodded in agreement. "OK the Oiler is due at 1600 hours, then the Lighter from Bull Point will be alongside at 0700 tomorrow, ammunitioning will commence straight away, every hand will be needed. I want the ammo onboard as quick as possible SAFELY!" Smiles and nudges around the cabin. "I don't know yet what we will be doing but as soon as I know I will pass it round. "No. 1, leave until 2200 hours. I guess this will be the last leave for some time. Coxswain go easy on the returners, they could be a little delicate!" Laughs all-round.

"Pilot, make sure you have all the charts required and check the Notifications are up-to-date. Mr. Vickers, you are now to assist the Pilot, go ashore and make sure all the confidential books are current. And tell your young lady goodbye!" The Midshipman tried to hide in a corner, looking bright red with embarrassment, the rest of the Officers hooted with laughter.

"That's all, carry on," Lee smiled, good to finish with a laugh!

The two tugs eased the ship away from the wall, and slowly headed downstream to The Sound, giving a blast on her fog horn to thank the dockyard and to let every other ship in the docks that 'Proud' *Preston* was going back to the war. The tannoy announced, "Hands attention on the upper deck, turn to port and salute Flag Officer Plymouth."

"Stand down."

Glasgow berthed nearby flashed, 'Good Luck'.

Out in The Sound, the tugs assisted *Preston* to do a compass swing, then she was cast off and she proceeded out of the breakwater, back to sea and the conflict.

"Pilot, set course for Lands' End, ring on 20 knots." The sea state was rising as the ship headed in to a force 7 sea.

"This will sort out the new crew!" commented Guns, with a wicked smile.

The sea rose to a full gale, and the ship had to slow down, so as not to receive storm damage. Around the ship many of the crew were incapacitated with seasickness, retching into buckets and getting no sympathy from the old salts! Round Lands' End and up the Bristol Channel, the ship had an uncomfortable rolling motion. Bridge telephone rang, OOW answers, "Sir, engine room for you."

"Yes, chief."

"Captain, we have a leak in the port shaft, it's right up against the gland space, I need to stop the port shaft to fix it."

"Damn we didn't need this, Chief. How long for repairs?"

Chief Engineer sucked in, "About five hours, sir. It's right by the bulkhead, sorry it didn't come to light during the trials."

"OK, Chief, quick as you can."

Lee turned, "OOW, ship to action stations, swing out the boats, everybody to wear life jackets, this is not a good place to be slowing down right in the middle of the Western Approaches."

As the alarm rattlers sounded, *Preston* slowed down and the pitching and rolling got worse.

Six hours later the Chief entered the bridge, "Ready to proceed with the port engine, sir. Sorry, it took longer than we thought."

"Thanks Chief, give my thanks to your Black Crew," Lee replied. "OOW, ring on port engine speed 15 knots, stand down action stations, normal watch routine." The reaction was palpable, and the air of tension disappeared, thank god they could proceed. Even the sea had calmed down, so soon the ship was at 25 knots, with the bone in her teeth, to passing vessels in the Irish Sea she would look magnificent. All departments were training hard, they needed to be ready for Scapa.

Entering Scapa, through the Fleet entrance at the Flotta Boom, and proceeding into the Flow, they turned to port and the rapidly expanding base at Lyness came into view. Picking up the buoy, and ringing off main engines, the Duty Oiler arrived alongside.

"Action stations!" The alarm sounds. "Air Raid Red!" Aircraft were approaching from the East.

The gun battery on South Ronaldsway opened fire, 'crump crump'. Looking aft, Lee watched as his 4in Guns sniffed the sky for the enemy. "DCT... Bridge, permission to open fire!"

"Granted. Firing bells, 'ting, ting', 'crack'!

A flight of 4 Ju88 bombers screamed towards the ship, two peeled off and headed towards the airfield at Hatston, the other two head towards the Battleship *Valiant*.

The range was closing fast and the pom-poms and 20mm joined in the racket! Another salvo from the 4in and incredibly it hit one of the Ju 88, its wing flying off and it dived into the Flow. Lee was speechless. Now the other Ju88 dropped its bombs alongside *Valiant* and headed over Hoy and away to sea, chased by bursting shells.

"*Valiant* signalling, sir, 'My bird I think'."

"No reply," orders Lee, "Guns, well done, bloody good shooting, pass the word to your crews, and ignore *Valiant*." Well, what a welcome.

After three exhausting weeks of work up, the ship was declared ready for deployment. A lot of the new crew had settled in very well and Lee was pleased with their progress, allowing the crew some liberty on Hoy and at the Fleet Canteen at Lyness, where a large fight between *Preston*'s and *Valiant*'s crews over the ownership of the shot down Junkers ensued. Lee was led to believe *Preston* won.

Lee watched as 'his' Walrus landed in the Flow and taxied over to the ship's side. Having been away for three weeks, based at Hatston, the crew had been on anti-submarine patrols and was now coming home. "OK, once the fly boys are aboard, we will get underway for Glasgow. No.1, pass the word, leaving harbour in thirty minutes"

Through the floating boom, and across the Pentland Firth, turning to starboard across the top of Scotland, the sea was again rough and the ship rolled badly, then onward down The Minches, before entering the Firth of Clyde, *Preston* anchored at The Tail 'o the Bank. A drifter came alongside with the ship's mail and their orders. The crew would be very happy for the mail, it had been missing for weeks.

HMS Jersey and *Jaguar* arrived shortly after Preston's escorts had arrived.

Chapter 3

The new orders were to escort a fast troop convoy as far as Gibraltar. There he was to load personnel and important equipment, from there to enter the Mediterranean, deliver to Malta, then as quickly as possible proceed to Alexandria. He was not to refuel at Malta unless it was absolutely necessary, owing to the shortage of fuel at Malta. Things had changed a lot in the past six months, the Med was no longer the quiet backwater, it was at the centre of the maelstrom of war. The German Afrika Corp had landed in North Africa and was fast approaching Egypt. The 8th Army had been moved from North Africa to Greece on Churchill's orders, to fight the Italian and German invasion, very much against the Army's wishes.

Proceeding across the Bay of Biscay at 20 knots, *Preston*, *Jersey* and *Jaguar* was joined by an anti-aircraft cruiser *Delhi*, another WW1 warship recalled to the flag, converted just before the war started, into an AA ship. She now packs a significant punch. Also, four sleek new Tribal class destroyers joined from Plymouth. The Admiralty obviously did not want to lose any of these troop ships! Under cloudless skies they proceeded south, nothing to disturb the journey. The new radar scanned the area around the ship for any threats, Lee was impressed at what he had seen of this new gadget so far.

"Nearly a pleasure cruise, No. 1. Let's hope it stays this way." Matley nodded, he did not want any trouble on this trip, he had a few issues with some of the new men he needed to sort out.

"Can I run a damage control exercise, sir?" Lee nodded.

Alf Matley had been recently promoted to First Lieutenant on an 'H' class destroyer, *HMS Handy*. Joining Warburton-Lee destroyer flotilla, they had entered the fjord that led to the Norwegian port of Narvik. Here they had encountered a larger, and better armed group of German destroyers, which outnumbered them by two to one. In the finest traditions of the Royal Navy, they attacked straight away, inflicting heavy losses on the Germans. However, they didn't have it all their own way. *Handy* was hit by a shell on the bridge, which wiped out everyone on there, apart from Matley. With the steering jammed she ran aground, and was hit repeatedly by the remaining German ships. The crew, that were left, were rescued by their flotilla mate *Hotspur* and returned to the UK. Matley was too junior to be given a command just yet, so had been sent to join *Preston*. Unfortunately, the demons kept coming, every time he closed his eyes.

Nearing the Straits, the radar picked up two ships approaching from the East. "Bunts, ask *Zulu* to investigate."

Lee watched as *Zulu* accelerated away in a flurry of foam, quickly rising to 30 knots, gosh they looked good at speed.

Moments later *Zulu* called up, *Dragon* and *Danae* approaching. Good, they were the reliefs, "Tell them to take their stations." After taking over, *Preston*, *Jersey*, *Jaguar* and *Delhi* were able to head for Gibraltar.

Just as dawn was rising, the four ships entered the harbour, far busier than the last time he was here, and Lee was struggling to get *Preston* to her berth near the dry docks. During the manoeuvre the signal station called, "*Preston* to report to the Admiral as soon as possible." Could have waited till they'd docked!

The tunnels were the same as last time, people rushing around with pieces of paper, but the armed guards were more in evidence than before. Entering the conference room, Lee was surprised to see other captains, and Admiral J Somerville RN, officer in charge of Force H.

"Now we are all here," the Dock Admiral sarcastically said, "We will begin." Clearly, no one told him about this conference, so he was struggling to catch-up.

"Smoke, gentlemen, if you wish! OK this will be Operation Ironman, departing in two days' time at 0300. The aim, is to pass ships through to Malta, then onto Cunningham at Alexandria. *Preston*, *Jaguar* and *Jersey* are to load RAF personnel, spare gun barrels, aircraft engines and ammunition for Malta. When offloaded, you will leave as soon as possible for Alexandria.

"Force H will depart earlier, so our friends in Spain can see them," (chuckles all round), "and will proceed towards Corsica, where a bombardment of the airfield there will be undertaken. This hopefully will draw the enemy attention to the north and not looking for anybody else. *Preston*, *Jersey* and *Jaguar*, any problems with your ships, get them sorted asap, and stay behind. Questions?" Discussions about timing, fuel etc. went on for another hour, finally the rest of the Captains were dismissed.

"OK, gather round." Admiral Somerville, waved to the three captains to come closer. "Gentlemen, your trip is vital for Malta's survival, since the Germans have shown up and we think they plan to take Malta for themselves. If we can retain it, we have a good chance of turning the tide. The air raids are taking a dreadful toll on the population and servicemen. We are planning a large scale operation soon, but we need to bring some respite to the island now.

"I had wanted to retain all three of you here, but ABC is struggling for ships in Alexandria, and I think he will have a major problem in Greece very soon, so that's why you are going there."

"Are your ships in good order?" Three heads nodded in agreement. "Good, there are some captured Italian BREDA 20mm guns, we will have them fitted to your ships, they may help, also ammunition to go with them. I am afraid you will have to man them from your ship's company.

"Carry on, try to give the ship's company as much rest as they can, I suspect they are going to need it." And with that he left the room with his Flag Lieutenant.

The next day, 'Force H' heads out to sea, *Ark Royal, Renown, Barham, Sheffield* and seven 'F' class destroyers. Making sure of a good display, they headed east into the Mediterranean. Right on cue the watchers in Spain, noted the departure. A message rushed across the ether, "Force H at sea, eastbound."

As Force H proceeded east then north, Somerville was conscious that he had to be spotted early enough, so deliberately passed within sight of the Balearic Islands. On paper his force looked impressive, but he knew better. *Renown* is fast, but her armour was paper thin, and would struggle in a gunnery brawl. *Barham* was slow, and badly in need of a refit. *Ark Royal* was good, but short of modern aircraft and pilots, her fighters were struggling against the modern Italian aircraft, but he knew he would need luck for this operation.

North and east, they plodded on. The destroyers were thrown out as a screen in the front of the fleet's advance. Swordfish aircraft on patrol, searched for the enemy. Onwards to Corsica, still not spotted, the Italians must be asleep. Hours later the few Swordfish were launched to bomb the airfield at Ajaccio, as *Renown, Barham, Sheffield* and two destroyers shot up the port of Ajaccio and the coastal railway line. Satisfied, the force re-joined the carrier and remaining destroyers and headed southwards. Somerville thought it was a complete waste of time. Three hours after leaving Corsican waters, a lone Italian Cant 505 aircraft was spotted, after a few minutes, it turned tail and headed home.

The following evening, in total silence and strictly black out enforced, *Preston*, *Jersey* and *Jaguar*, left the Rock. Loaded with as many supplies as possible, and mess decks crowded with RAF personnel. Lee had ordered that they stay below, he didn't want them spotted. Fortunately, they were not spotted, the smoke floats had been activated on the detached mole, and this obscured their departure. Heading east at a leisurely pace, they struck lucky with the sea state, a nice gentle state 2. Spare hands had been found for the Italian guns, and the ammunition for them was everywhere, causing Lee a few worries. The sooner they could offload the supplies, the sooner he could stow the ammo better.

As dawn broke, they had worked up to 20 knots, trying to make distance but conscious of the need to conserve fuel. Having spoken to *Jersey* and *Jaguar*, they reported this was their ideal speed. The weather was stunning, deep blue sea, and a rich blue sky, not a cloud in sight.

Lee turned to Beddall, "Beautiful day, Guns, if this was cruise liner, I would be very happy, but we are not, and we can be spotted for miles, I don't like it."

Turning to the Navigator Lt Watson RNR, "Pilot did you get all the charts updated, for minefields etc.?"

"Yes, sir, we have also got the new position of the field laid by *Manxman* two days ago."

"Good, how's you assistant doing?"

After twenty years on various merchant ships, Watson had travelled the seven seas, so navigation came easy for him, but he was annoyed. He should have taken command of his first ship, a tanker, before being called back to the Colours. So, he was taking his anger out, unfairly on Vickers, "He's getting there, sir."

As the day passed, and the warm sun made men drowsy, Matley called for a damage control exercise, flood in the stoker's mess. That woke everybody up, might as well keep them busy.

At noon "Radar... Bridge, aircraft steering 090 degrees 30 miles out."

"Action stations." Alarms go off, and men rush to their places. All eyes span ahead to search for anything flying.

Lookout. "Got her, sir, biplane just of the starboard bow."

"DCT... Bridge, got her, she's a Spanish commercial aircraft from North Africa to Spain."

Damn hissed Lee, could have done without him seeing us. In theory he should not report our position, but I bet he will! "OK, OOW, once he is out of range stand the men down. No. 1, pilot, and Guns, navigation cabin, please."

"OK, gentleman, suggestions? Do we continue, do we change course, or do we return to Gib?" The options seemed many, and after thirty minutes of discussion, it was decided to alter course for the North African coast, but still head for Malta. This was passed to the destroyers, who agreed.

By nightfall they were abreast Algiers, which stood out in the darkness, no blackout here! On into the night, the whoosh of water, the roar of the engine room fans, the scrape of ammunition belts on steel, the whispering of sailors. All was well, so far. Lee retired to his sea cabin to get some sleep; he was going to be busy in the next few days so needed to get some rest.

Timmins, his servant, awoke him with a cup of tea, "Sir, thirty minutes to sun up."

"Thanks, Timmins." Picking up the phone. "Report."

"OOW, sir, hands at action station, nothing on radar or in sight, speed 20 knots and we are twenty miles off the African coast."

"Very good, on my way up." Good God, he had slept through dawn action stations! That will never do!

A moment later he was on the bridge, everybody was at their station, and all was quiet. "Anything in the log about last night No. 1?"

"Nothing, sir."

"Very good, ask Mr Jones to come to the bridge at 1000 hours and bring his fuel calculation table with him. Also, we will go to action stations at 1300, but let the men relax at their station it's going to be a long, few days. Alf, if you could have a wander around the ship, make sure all is well, thanks."

At 1000 Jones appeared. "Hi Chief, just to see how you are doing, and can you give me an update on fuel consumption?"

They chatted for a while, and Lee was happy with what he heard. Thank goodness Jonesy was old school, he liked him, and wished he could meet him more regularly, and nothing seemed to faze him.

He contacted the destroyers and informed them he would be going to action stations when they were abreast El Kala at about 1300. They were doing fine; the two destroyer Captains were regulars and appeared on their game.

As they passed El Kala, they deployed paravanes, increased speed to 25 knots and headed towards the Sicilian Narrows, then the Skerki passage, staying close to the Skerki bank, avoiding the known minefield, they headed towards Cape Bon and Pantelleria. Dusk was just starting.

"Radar… Bridge, aircraft bearing due north forty miles."

"Very good, pass the word."

The Italian Cant 505 was nearing the end of its patrol area, and was about to turn back when something glinted on the horizon, so he decided to have a look. Just as the sun was setting, they spotted a cruiser and two destroyers at speed near Cape Bon heading east. Not getting within gun range, they headed for their base, sending out a sighting report as she sped away.

Lee ordered, "Chief Yeoman, see if you can jam the signals from that plane. Damn, pity we were spotted, I guess it's going to be busy tomorrow, standdown action stations and set state 2."

Chapter 4

The ship was at dawn action stations, the air was hot and humid, with little breeze, closed up in anti-flash gear the crew were already wringing wet. The lookouts scanned the horizon, and the radar repeater showed clear. Lee was just about to standdown, when a lookout called, "Many aircraft to the north east."

"Well done, Ash!"

"Radar... Bridge, set not working sir!"

"Bloody Hell!"

The 10 Cant 505 bombers droned on towards them, having left their base at 0300, they were hoping to catch the ships as dawn broke, but they were late. Set up in a large airborne circle, they attacked from sun up, from the west.

"DCT open fire when in range." Bang! The 6in guns opened fire at maximum elevation, and kept up a steady barrage. As the aircraft got closer, the high angle 4inch and the Pom-poms opened fire.

The aircraft began their attack, flying straight down the line of advance, they dropped their bombs together. Lee ordered, "Hard a port." *Preston* and the destroyers turned together. "Tell the destroyers to act independently." The bombs started falling, all down the starboard side about 500 yards away. They then split up and attacked individually, all missing by a wide margin, which brought shouts of derision from the gun crews. However, one of the Cants was shot down, and one was seen low over the water trailing black smoke. "Good shooting, Guns. Slow to 15 knots, and hoist in the paravanes, and tell the destroyers to resume station." Operation completed, they resumed course for Malta at 25 knots.

Clear off the Sicilian Narrows, and past the fortress on Pantelleria, they headed north east for Malta,

Radar reported the set was working again, so Lee relaxed. Shortly followed by the report, "Four ships bearing 025, range 45 miles." Here we go again. "Ask the fly-boys to take a looksee," Lee ordered. Fifteen minutes later, the Walrus was airborne and the range had dropped to 42 miles.

"Sir, aircraft reports two light cruiser of the *Giussano* class and two destroyers, one of the cruisers is trailing oil."

"Very good, sound action stations, surface action, hoist battle ensigns, ask the plane to report fall of shot. Full speed ahead. Maybe the Engineer can now show us what the ship can really do!"

No. 1 stepped forward, and quietly said, "Sir, is this a good idea, with all this ammo and passengers onboard?"

"Unfortunately, No. 1, they are between us and Valletta. Tell *Jersey* and *Jaguar* to take independent action, concentrate on the Italian destroyers, and if they get a chance, a torpedo attack on the cruisers. Contact the Admiralty, tell them we are engaging the enemy, DCT range?" "Still too far away."

Picking up the phone Lee called the engine room, "Eric I need every bit of power, we are in a chase for some eyetie cruisers."

"Will do, sir, let's see if we can break *Latona's* speed claims!"

A tense thirty minutes later, *Preston*, really has the bone between her teeth, and the range had come down significantly, "They don't appear to have seen us, the lookouts should be on a fizzer!" OOW states.

"Guns, open fire when you can." As the range dropped down rapidly. 'A' and 'B' turret fired the first salvo.

"Over, down 100."

"Shoot."

"Down 50."

"Shoot." Straddle!

Guided by the Walrus, *Preston* concentrated on the nearest destroyer, she hits her amidships, she slowed down. Shifted target to the rear cruiser. At last, the Italians reacted, and started to lay a smoke screen and they fired the first shots at Lee. The shots fell astern, but one close to the port quarter. With the airplane's assistance, *Preston* found the range and hit the cruiser with another salvo. Onboard the *Pisa* the four shells had caused chaos, nos. 2 and 3 boiler rooms were flooding, aft engine room hit and the port turbine was out of action, as were both rear turrets, the rudder was jammed, and her speed had dropped. They started to list to starboard. As *Preston* surged past, battle ensigns standing out in the breeze, she fired three full salvos at *Pisa*. Lightly built, the *Giussano* class are built for speed and she suffered badly from the British gunfire. Now stopped, her crew in disarray, the ship was doomed. *Jersey*, after finishing of the *Lupo*, fired a salvo of torpedoes at *Pisa*, which hit the bow and engine room and she quickly rolled over and sank.

Now it was a stern chase. On paper, *Milan* was faster than *Preston*, but nobody counted on Jonesy! With 'the bone in her teeth', *Preston* surged forward. Slowly the range dropped as the ship got up to 35 knots, guided by the ship's spotter airplane, *Preston* landed two hits on *Milan*, one on the bridge and the other on 'B' gundeck, chaos as the command structure was eliminated on *Milan*. No one wanted to take control. *Preston* turned to starboard and fired broadside after broadside at *Milan*. Like *Pisa*, she was not built to take punishment, and literally came apart, slowly sinking by the bow.

Jersey and *Jaguar* concentrated on *Spica*, but she was too fast for the British warships, and chased by long range fire from *Preston*, she escaped to the north west, badly damaged.

Lee couldn't believe it, what a victory! Splinter damage aft on the quarter-deck and 'Y' turret, and three men injured, none serious. *Jersey* hit by two 4.1-inch shells, damage light and *Jaguar* reported no damage! "Recall the Walrus and clean the ship up and resume course for Malta."

He thought, I must go around the ship and thank everybody, but I can't leave the bridge yet, we are still in danger. Maybe when we have unloaded. The Chief called, "Sir, we used a bit more fuel than anticipated, because of the chase, we will be marginal at Malta, also the destroyers are low."

"OK, Chief Yeoman, send message to the Admiralty repeated VA Malta and Force H, we will require fuel on arrival Malta, due to recent action, have it coded and timed, Bunts."

The Buffer, comes to the bridge, "Have a word sir?"

"Yes, Buff what can I do for you?"

"The hit aft was in the wardroom pantry, and it was taking in water faster than the pumps could handle, we were unable to staunch the flow of water, due to the wave created by the ship's speed."

"OK."

"Leading Seaman Atkinson, from the Aft Damage Control Party, managed to gain entry to the compartment, sized up the problem, and fixed it."

"OK, Buffer, what was special about that?"

"Sir, he sat with his arse in the shell hole, keeping the flow of water down until the pumps could contain the leak and had emptied the compartment. Sir he is now in sickbay suffering from exposure, he was there for two hours."

"Bloody hell, No. 1, that takes some stamina, thanks Buff, I will see he gets some recognition for his efforts."

It was nearly nightfall as *Preston* continued onward, the recon Cant had been following for the past two hours, and Lee was fully expecting a reprisal air raid for the loss of those warships. Sure enough, they arrived like avenging demons, SM79's nickname the 'hunchback', tri-engine bombers, made repeated attacks on all three ships, dodging and weaving, they raced on, the destroyers repeatedly disappearing amongst bomb splashes. The twilight sky was lit up by multicoloured tracer rounds, they crisscrossed the sky searching for a target. These were not the same pilots as this morning, these were far better. Just as the last light faded *Jersey* was hit on 'A' gun by a bomb.

"*Jersey* on fire, sir."

Lee replied, "Ask *Jaguar* to standby her. Cox'n slow to 15 knots, hard port rudder, we will circle round and see if we can help."

By the time the ship had circled back, *Jersey* called up to say she was ready to proceed, bulkheads shored up and the fire nearly out, some casualties amongst the RAF personnel.

Chapter 5

Onward to Malta, speed 15 knots. One of the lookouts reported something in the water. It looked like a RAF pilot in a one-man raft. *Preston* slowed to pick him up. On collection, he was a young German Air Gunner. He was looked after and put in the ship's cells for now.

Using Malta as cover, they proceeded to the south of the island then, around the east side to enter Valletta. *Preston* signalled, 'One German POW onboard will swap for potatoes'. The signal came back, 'We have plenty of POWs but no potatoes'. That made everyone laugh.

Signs of past air-raids showed on the battlements, and the odd sunken wreck cluttered the harbour. *Jersey* was taken straight into No. 1 drydock for repairs to commence immediately, even while she was being unloaded. *Preston* was moved against the west wall of No. 5 dock, where an army of stevedores swarmed aboard, and a fuel lighter was dragged alongside. Above, the Italian air force watch and wait. Five hours later, *Preston* and *Jaguar* were ready to leave. *Jersey* would have to stay in the drydock at Malta, she was badly damaged after the bomb strike.

Just then the Italians were back, more SM 79s. Every gun around the Grand Harbour opened fire, with

Preston and *Jaguar* both adding weight to the barrage. Two Hurricanes dived down through the shell fire and chased away some of the bombers, but too little, too late. A string of bombs landed across *Jersey*, blowing her sideways off the blocks in the drydock, and setting fire to her, she would never leave Malta. With the withdrawal of the Italian planes, and aided by tugs, *Preston* was turned in the harbour, and following *Jaguar* slowly out past the breakwater, set course for Alexandria. As they increased speed, a huge explosion about two hundred yards off *Jaguar*'s portside, rocked *Preston* — an influence mine! *Jaguar* reported only light damage. Thank goodness for that, thought Lee.

Next morning, the Regia Aeronautica attacked again, but this was, without doubt, the 'B' team, and the bombs landed far away. The persistent shadower stayed with them, going around and around.

Lee said, "Bunts, signal that aircraft and ask them to go around the other way they are making me dizzy."

"Aye, sir. No reply, sir, miserable sod!" That was the last incident before they reached Alexandria.

Two days later, they were approaching through the swept channel and 'The Narrows'. *Preston* passed first the breakwater and then the boom.

No. 1 reported, "Sir, all the ships have their sides manned, what the…!" As they approached the first ship, the harbour erupted in cheering, every ship was cheering *Preston* and *Jaguar*. The 'bunting tossers' were overwhelmed by the messages of congratulations and best wishes. But above all on the fleet flagship *Warspite*, the signal, 'Manoeuvre well executed!'

Reaching their berth, the crew walked around the ship with huge smiles on their faces, Lee was so proud of them all!

Warspite signalled '*Preston* and *Jaguar* repair onboard.' Off to see Cunningham then.

As tradition dictateed, Lee was first aboard with *Jaguar*'s Captain following. With awnings spread, a fully turned out side party, bosuns calls twittering, and a Royal Marine band assembled. Jackson, *Jaguar*'s skipper, looked overwhelmed. Lee smiled at him, "It will be fine, it's not a court martial," they both laughed. Coming towards them was Admiral A B Cunningham, with a big smile and his hand out, dispensing with ceremony he vigorously shook Lee's then Jackson's hand. "Well done, bloody well done, that gave the eyetie's a bloody nose, what!" (A.B.C. as he is known to the Fleet, was a sailor's sailor, loved by his men and a scourge to the enemy. He would not take any nonsense from anybody, had clashed with Churchill on a few occasions, and did not suffer fools gladly.) Escorted to the Admiral's cabin, he lavishly entertained them, as they repeated the minute-by-minute account of the action, asking searching questions, and with his Flag Lieutenant furiously scribbling down notes. After lunch, and satisfied he had all the answers, they relaxed over a glass of gin and ABC explained what the picture was in the Eastern Med.

"The army is struggling in Greece, I told Winston not to send them over there, but he insisted, now they are being pushed back to the coast. I suspect in the next day or two we will have to go and get them. In North Africa, the Germans and Italians have now succeeded in building up enough supplies, that I think they could be pushing towards us and the Canal soon. The Fascist backed government in Syria and the Levant are also flexing their muscles. I am short of ships and supplies, as you know it all has to be hauled round the Cape, which takes time. It's a pity we lost *Jersey*, we could have done with another modern destroyer, and Malta being bombed so regularly, it's virtually neutralised it. I want to give both ship's company forty-eight hours leave, they deserve it, but before that ammunition and refuel, and again well done." With that they were dismissed.

Hours later, the gangway was packed with sailors, dressed in their uniform whites, they all wanted to visit the delights of Alexandria. As CPO Mason inspected the crew, he was issuing dire warnings about the loose women, and the lowlife who would like nothing better than to rob a poor matelot. "And finally, leave finishes at 2200 hours, make sure you are back on time, and if anybody comes back onboard with the clap, its two weeks in the 'Rose Garden' then on report for a self-inflicted injury, so be warned." Sniggers and nudges all-round, and the first section of liberty men happily left the ship. Watching from the bridge wing, Lee and Matley smiled. Lee said, They are eager to go ashore, they deserve it, you going ashore No. 1?"

"No, sir, there's nothing in this dump that interests me, I will get some paintings done." Lee had found out that Matley was a very accomplished landscape artist.

"Right if you need me, I will be in my cabin, I am off to attack all that paperwork again!" groaned Lee.

"Good luck, sir."

In the Officer's Only room, in a bar downtown, Messrs Beddall, Jones and Watson, were having a quiet drink and chat, just to get away from the ship for a few precious hours. The room next door, for ratings, was noisy. A party of *Preston* men entered, to cat calls and banter, here they are, the 'glory hunters', and other derogatory remarks. Which brought the inevitable brawl, glasses and fists flying everywhere, tables and chairs crashing to the floor, bystanders scurrying for safety. After a few moments, it was all over, and before the Navy's shore patrol arrived, a leading hand from 'B' gun stood with his other victorious mates, and declared, "We are the 'Proud *Prestons*', and don't you lot forget it!" Then a mass stampede for the exits, as the bar emptied in record time. Moment later the Shore Patrol turned up, to an empty bar. The only matelots left were the unconscious ones on the floor, who were rounded up and unceremoniously thrown in the back of a van.

The Officer in charge came up to the Chief, and asked him what happened, "I don't know we just arrived." The officer looked at the table covered with glasses, and stormed away.

Chapter 6

The next morning at defaulter table, a line of battered-looking sailors looked at the Captain. Immensely proud of his men, Lee tried not to smile, he should deal with them one by one, but looking at the line, it would take ages. After the charges were read out, Lee spoke, "Right all guilty, loss of one day's leave, today's date, one day's loss of pay. Cox'n, stand them down."

"Sir, right turn, on caps, march!" The men left the quarterdeck. Lee knew that he was being watched from various telescopes on the Flag Ship.

"Sir, that was very lenient of you," commented No. 1.

"I know, but how can you punish men like these, most of them will be on watch today so a loss of leave isn't going to hurt them and the day's pay is enough punishment! Did you hear, they call themselves, *Proud Prestons*!" Lee smiled.

Forty-eight hours later, *Preston* was ready for sea, Lee had his orders. He, along with two destroyers, were to escort four merchantmen, from the Port Suez to Haifa. Clearing the boom, they increased speed and established cruising stations. It took about four hours to Port Said, and as they approached the Canal entrance Lee was happy to see the merchant ships leaving harbour, amidst clouds of funnel smoke. Lee looked across at Watson, who was shaking his head with embarrassment, "Lord help us," mutters Watson. "That smoke can be seen for miles."

"Pilot, let's hope it's not one of your old berth's."

Watson shook his head, "No, sir, I wouldn't allow it, it's the results of ship owners not spending money on maintenance before the war began, unfortunately it's the crews who pay the cost. Sir, did you know that your pay finishes the moment your ship gets sunk, and any expenses are yours till you get another ship? Not the way to treat heroes." Lee was truly shocked, this was information he did not know.

Lee watched, as these smoky, rust-streaked ships were ushered into cruising positions by the destroyers. With what Watson had said, he looked on these crews with a new respect.

They headed north up the coast of the Holy Land, passing Tel Aviv. Haifa came into view with an escorting trawler waiting at the entrance to greet them. Lee ordered the two destroyers in to harbour to top off with fuel. *Preston* then cruised up and down the coast as the destroyers went about their business.

Back together, they set course for Greek waters. At a steady pace, they passed close to Cyprus and then into the Aegean Sea. Closing up, anti-aircraft guns crew and extra lookout were posted, the radar eye scanning all around them. Lee wanted to be ready.

Chief Yeoman spoke, "Message sir, proceed with all dispatch too Piraeus, and start loading troops."

"Thank you, Pilot, plot me a course."

As ABC had predicted, the situation in Greece had turned into a disaster, the army was in full retreat to Athens and other south coast ports, and needed to be evacuated. Threading her way through the islands in the Aegean, towards Piraeus at full speed, the destroyers keeping pace with him, he was pleased to see their crews closed up action stations. "Radar... Bridge aircraft approaching from the North East 20 plus." As they came through the passage between Kimilos and Sifnos, the aircraft started to circle about forty miles away, and started attacking a convoy of ships.

"It's not us they are after," muttered Watson, as they watched as aircraft after aircraft fell from the sky to attack, then climbed up, to circle around, and attack again. Two ships were sinking and black dots littered the sky as the escort tried to fight off the enemy. "Radar... Bridge, aircraft heading back to land,"

"Very good, standby to rescue survivors." The ship slowed down and scrambling nets were deployed.

"No. 1, I am not stopping, so make sure you are as quick as you can be."

"Bunts ask the Escort leader what he wants from us."

"*Hotspur* signalling, can we collect the men to the south of us in the water, he says, he can manage the rest."

"Will do."

Proceeding at slow speed, he collected the group of men in the water. Unfortunately, there were not many, mostly army personnel, and a few sailors. It doesn't take long, and the crew breathed a sigh of relief as Lee ordered the speed increased and headed toward the coast.

"*Hotspur* signalling, 'thanks'."

"Acknowledge."

Collecting *Hercules* and *Hero* his two destroyers, he headed for Piraeus.

As they approached, there were numerous fires in the town, and the acrid smell of burning was everywhere. Directed to go alongside the jetty, Lee manoeuvred the ship so she was pointing towards the entrance, ready for a quick getaway. The jetty was full of soldiers, with NCOs rushing around to keep them in order. As the brow went down, a harassed looking Lt Cdr, rushed onboard. Presenting himself to the bridge, he brought orders. 'Load as many as you can, take them to Crete, Suda Bay, offload and return as quickly as possible'.

"No. 1, get the Cox'n to organise the soldiers onboard. Get as many below decks as you can, sharp about it."

Lee watched from the bridge as the men streamed onboard. It was easy to spot the different regiments, the disciplined and the unruly. Message from the gangway,

'We have some sailors from *Venom*, sunk a few days ago, can we take them onboard?'

"Yes, allocate them to messes as appropriate." The bedraggled sailors came up the gangway, with nothing but what they stood up in. Two hours later Matley reported to the bridge, "Sir, with the survivors from the convoy, and what we have loaded today, we have 2,580 extra souls onboard. I have moved as many as I can below, but the naval ratings want to help, so I have put them to good use. The gun decks have been left clear, in case we have to fight the ship, heaven help us if we do."

"Well done."

Preston got underway, but she was sluggish, all the extra souls were weighing her down. Collecting *Hercules* and *Hero*, they made their way out of the harbour. Both destroyers had about 800 soldiers onboard each. Heading south, and the sea was rising, again the three ships, started to butt into the sea. The Aegean was not kind to them, as they struggled with the extra people onboard. They cleared the headland, and the seas increased and Lee was forced to slow down, the ships were struggling. "Radar… Bridge, unidentified aircraft approaching from the west."

"Action Stations!" Lee scanned the horizon, there they were, but they looked different?

"DCT… Bridge, 20 plus Junkers 88s." That's why they looked different.

"Guns open fire when you can. Ask the destroyers to lay smoke. Battle bowlers, everyone."

The six-inch battery opened fire first, at maximum elevation. The ear-splitting roar as they went off. The aircraft kept coming. Salvo after salvo until the main battery could elevate no more, and had to cease fire. The twin, four-inch now took up the challenge, the noise was terrific, the smell of cordite everywhere, still they kept coming. The Junkers now started their attack dives, the Pom-poms and 20mm. now opened fire. Tracers bullets zipped across the sky. Lee conned the ship, this way and that, still mindful of the sluggishness of his command. *Hero* disappeared, surrounded by water spouts, but emerged unscathed, spitting fire, *Hercules* was weaving, in an attempt to throw the pilots off their game. Lee looked aft and watched as his gunner's loaded and fired continuously, aided by the extra sailors taken onboard, there were ample men for the extra guns.

"DCT... Bridge, enemy withdrawing, can confirm the loss of two aircraft."

"Thanks, Guns, but they will be back. OOW, report damage."

Back on course and with ammunition having been replaced, the crews were ready. They were back, another 10 Ju 88s, same pattern as before. The guns commenced, the terrific noise, ship swerving to miss dropping bombs, then silence as aircraft droned away. Again, replenished ammunition, cleared up the empty brass cases.

Exhausted men sat and rested for a short time. Fortunately, again no hits, they had been very lucky.

"Ask the cooks to supply the crew with action messing, get some of those soldiers to help."

One of the Army officers came to the bridge, and saluted Lee. "Can my men help, sir, we have plenty of Lewis and Bren guns available."

"Thank you, Major, my Gunner will tell you where to position you men." Beddall and the Major left the bridge. Lee sat in his chair, he was exhausted and his left leg was shaking. Just then Timmins came on the bridge, with a tray of corn beef sandwiches and a cup of coffee. "Timmins, you're a life-saver.", Lee didn't realize how hungry he was, and wolfed down the sandwiches.

"Air raid, thirty plus aircraft, approaching from the east." Just as the sun was setting, here we go again. Gun crews and the additional soldiers stood ready. The six-inch open fire, then in a staggered order, the rest. Again, tracer rounds lit up the twilight sky. *Hero* was straddled by bombs, her side pierced by shrapnel, she slowed down. Dodging and weaving, *Preston* and *Hercules* circled *Hero*, their gunfire trying to protect her. Lee observed two bombers crash into the sea, and a third fly low down the port side smoking badly. This was too much for the frustrated pongos, who opened withering fire on the stricken bomber, literally tearing it to pieces. The daylight had now gone, *Hero* reported she could proceed but only at 15 knots. Fortunately, the sea had lost much of its venom. On towards Crete, ship's crew and passengers, again replaced used ammunition, and exhausted guns crews tried to get some rest.

Lee retired to his sea cabin, he sat at his desk, but immediately fell asleep, head resting on his arms. Timmins entered a couple of hours later, to see the Captain, head back in his chair, mouth open, snoring gently, he was going to waken him, but decided that he would leave it a while. He sat by the telephone, ready to intercept it, so his Captain could rest. Around him the ship went about its business; every turn of the screws took her closer to Crete.

Dawn action stations. Weary men stood by the guns, some men slept soundly, others fitfully and a few had no sleep at all. So, the men of *Preston* got ready for another angry day.

On the bridge, Lee was in his chair, everybody was closed up ready for the enemy. The ship was now heading west, directly away from the rising sun. The lookouts scanning the sky, Radar reported no contacts. Everybody was tired after the action yesterday, and looking for some rest. Now turning to the south towards Suda, the enemy arrived, and in some force. As yesterday, the attack was in waves with some high-level bombing others as dive bombers. The ships dodged and weaved, but *Hero* was struggling, Lee conned the ship to be between the aircraft and *Hero*. Lee ordered *Hercules* to head for Suda to disembark her passengers. Again, *Hero* was straddled, she started to slow down, and yet again the ship was hit by shrapnel, causing casualties amongst her soldiers. The last three bombers attacked *Hero*, and a bomb hit 'X' gundeck, causing a huge explosion. 'X' gun flew up into the air, followed by the gun crew and soldiers. "Oh my God!" an angry shout from someone on the bridge. *Hero* slowed to a stop. The enemy disappeared over the horizon, with two aircraft smoking badly, a poor reward for the ships company. With Suda in sight, he ordered them to send assistance. But *Hero* was low in the water, so Lee had his ship's boats to be lowered to assist. *Hero*, by now, had been stabilised. Lee left the scene to discharge his soldiers. Heading to Suda, Lee was pleased to see a mixed fleet of fishing boats, tugs etc. all heading for *Hero*.

With *Preston* berthed, her passengers left the ship, but the mess they left behind was unbelievable. This was cleared in double time, and ammunition replaced. A few hours later, *Hero* was helped into the bay, surrounded by various trawlers, tugs, and *Preston*'s boats, which Lee was happy to see. His ship's boats were soon taken back onboard.

It was time to go back to Piraeus. *Preston* moved out of the bay, followed by *Hercules*, and working up to full speed, the ships handled better. "Air Raid, twenty enemy approaching from the north east." Here we go again.

Lee was going to try a new tactic, he turned towards the attackers, closing the range. Just as the aircraft started their dive, he turned hard astarboard, presenting his full broadside, and opened fire, this seemed to unsettle the pilots, who dropped early. Then hard aport and fired again, again upsetting the pilots. They broke off and headed home. Returning to his course for Piraeus, continued, still at full speed. Half way to their destination, they had another air-raid, this time it was the Italian SM 79s high level bombers, again these were not the A team, and the bombs went wide.

Approaching the port, the buildings surrounding the docks were ablaze, fires, smoke and explosions everywhere. Lee eased the ship against the jetty, and the waiting soldiers started scrambling onboard not waiting for the gangways to go down, chaos! *Hercules* was the same, soldiers everywhere trying to get onboard. "Air raid aircraft approaching." Lee looked aghast, he had seen these aircraft before at Dunkirk — Stukas! There was nothing he could do, he was tied up, with no manoeuvring room, it was down to his gun crews now. As the Stukas circled, they lined up in the air and peeled off one by one to attack, their sirens screamed, the sound of a Stuka. The guns roared a greeting, everybody was firing. Then the bombs landed, Poor *Hercules* took four hits, which tore her apart, decimating her crew. A merchant ship berthed just ahead of *Hercules* also got hit by two bombs and started to burn furiously. Bombs landed on the quayside amongst the waiting soldiers, carnage, bits of bodies flying everywhere. Two trucks laden with ammunition, near the merchant ship were also hit, and they erupted and added to the noise and chaos. His gun crews worked like demons, the 20mm gun barrels glowed red hot as they fired. Then the enemy were gone.

The sounds died down, and smoke drifted across the ship, the crackle of fire and the pop as bullets 'cooked off'. Cries and groans of injured men were everywhere. Mercifully, *Preston* was undamaged, a few hands had minor injuries, but the ship was covered in brick dust and burning embers. As fast as they could, they loaded the injured and uninjured alike. This was not the orderly embarkation of the last visit, this was a mob on the run, but he couldn't stay here, if he did, he knew he would lose the ship. Eventually, everyone who was in the dock area, were now onboard, it was time to go. Just as he was ready to cast off, an army truck came skidding to a halt, a party of WRENs were delivered to the ship, well, that will cheer the men up!

Orders from the Admiralty, were not to proceed to Suda but to go to Alexandria. Again, the ship was sluggish, but he headed south, then west for Egypt and Jonesy and his black gang gave him full speed. As she built up speed, Lee looked back. Piraeus was ablaze, two ships in the harbour entrance were on fire, both were struggling to get underway, a small tug trying to help. An old Greek destroyer was standing by to escort them. What a shambles. "Air raid aircraft approaching." Groans — not again.

"Engine room, all you've got, Chief." *Preston* surged forward. The aircraft approached Piraeus and started their deadly business again, over the port, leaving the ship alone.

On they steamed, the burning port disappeared in the distance. An Italian SM79 joined them, but did not attack and after a few hours, it turned away. They were left alone.

Lee turned over the bridge to Matley, and he headed down to do a quick inspection. Everywhere, exhausted soldiers, fast asleep, his crew were quietly going about their duties, but Lee could see their tiredness. With many injuries he had ordered the Walrus out of its hanger and the space was being used to treat the casualties. His Surgeon and SBA are covered in blood, but working away, WRENs helping out, no one noticed him watching. A line of bodies lay along the ships side, he would have to bury them soon, in this heat they would corrupt quickly. As dusk approached the ship slowed to bury her dead, a quick service was conducted, and twenty-seven men were committed to the deep. The common prayer being recited:

"O eternal Lord God who alone spreadest out the heavens and rulest the raging seas, who hast compassed the waters with bounds until night and day come to an end, be pleased to receive into thy Almighty and gracious protection the persons of us thy servants and the fleet in which we serve, Persevere us from the violence of the enemy."

A sadness descended on the ship, this was their first burial at sea. Speed increased, they continued to Alexandria.

As they approached Alexandria, ships were leaving in ones and twos, and as they passed *Preston,* they all cheered her, her decks packed with Khaki coloured soldiers, who looked on bemused. Lee was pleased to see the quayside lined with ambulances and Army 7-ton trucks to take away his passengers. They could recover from their ordeal.

Again, the ship's company had to clear up the mess the soldiers had left, bits of uniform, rifles, ammunition, empty bully beef cans, soiled bandages, etc. They had also eaten every bit of food onboard, so priority would be restocking with food, shells and fuel. Some minor damage was also being repaired by the Buffer and his men, assisted by a few dockyard personnel.

Chapter 7

Sealed orders arrive onboard, they were to proceed, along with *Calcutta*, *Hotspur* and *Hereward*. The ships were to constitute a strike force, to interdict the enemy ships that were sailing south from Greece to Crete carrying troops. Because of the enemy air superiority, they must be south of the island by daybreak. Caiques, coastal traders, tugs, barges, merchant ships and Italian warships were all heading south carrying troops and must be stopped. He was glad he had *Calcutta* with him. She had been converted into an anti-aircraft cruiser, just prior to the outbreak of war. *Hotspur* and *Hereward* were two 'H' class destroyers, good ships, but weak in anti-aircraft guns, he would have to keep an eye on them.

They left as the sun rose the next day. Heading towards Crete, they made leisurely progress, Lee wanted to get there tomorrow evening just as the sun set. Two Royal Navy Fulmar fighters circled the force as they proceeded. Later as their escort departed, Beddall turned to Watson, "Ha! there they go, home to tea, bed and medals."

"I still think I would like to be on here, feels so safe and secure" Watson replied.

"Sir, *Hotspur* reports submarine contact," Beddall leapt across the bridge, "Action stations, Captain to the bridge, increase speed to 25 knots, commence zig zag."

Moments later, Lee was in his chair, "Well done, Guns. Tell *Hereward* to assist *Hotspur*."

"*Hotspur* attacking."

"Thanks, Bunts."

The sea erupted behind *Hotspur*, then *Hereward* moved into attack, again explosions in the sea. "*Hotspur* reporting lost contact. *Hereward* never gained contact."

"Thanks, ask them to re-join, can't afford to hang around here."

The sea in the Mediterranean was notorious for its different underwater currents, freshwater mixing with saltwater and warm and cold layers, made sub hunting very difficult.

U51 sneaked away. He knew how lucky he was, the last attack had shaken them up badly, but still, they lived to fight another day. They headed north, where were those ships going?

The next day, an hour before dusk, Lee ordered the crew to change into clean underwear and to have some food, it's going to be a long night, Crete lay ahead. Now positioned in line ahead, *Hotspur* led, then *Preston*, *Calcutta* and *Hereward* bringing up the rear. They increased speed.

"Radar… Bridge four small contacts at thirty miles heading south." So, it began.

The DCT silently turned to seek out the targets. Moments later, "Contact, two small merchant ships, one ferry and a small warship"

Lee replied, "Guns, very good, we will take the warship, tell the destroyers to take on the merchant ships and *Calcutta* to sink the ferry."

The four-inch S1 mounting opened fire with a loud crack. (gun mountings on either side of the ship were numbered for the right, or starboard side S1 onwards, S1 being closest to the bow. On the Port or left side, they were numbered again from the bow P1 etc.). The starshell exploded over the enemy convoy, and it was exposed in a deathly white light, moments later all guns open fire. Within minutes, the four enemy ships were ablaze, the warship had desperately tried to interdict herself between the British warships and the convoy, but *Preston*'s six-in guns blew her apart. One of the merchant ships had a small gun on the stern and was trying to engage *Hereward*, but to no avail, it was hit and blasted overboard. In thirty minutes, it was all over, the strike force moved on, leaving four sinking ships behind them.

Further into the Aegean Sea they cruised on, they then came across five Caiques, all packed with German Mountain Troops, these were quickly dispatched to the deep. Moving on, yet another small convoy was encountered, but the escort of two Italian destroyers were fully awake, having heard the gunfire earlier. Starshells were fired as the convoy appeared out of the darkness. The Italians lay smoke to protect their charges. *Preston* and *Calcutta* engaged the destroyers, while *Hotspur* and *Hereward* proceeded around the smoke screen to attack the merchant ships.

Calcutta was hit on the bridge, but continued engaging the enemy, the two destroyers ran riot amongst the shipping. *Preston* hit one of the Italian destroyers, which, slowed down and started to sink. *Calcutta's* victim was lost in the darkness, she had stopped firing at *Calcutta*, and disappeared. Three merchant ships were torpedoed by the *Hotspur* and *Hereward*, and a fourth, riddled by gunfire. The rest scattered amongst the islands, although two were badly damaged.

It was now three in the morning, and Lee was aware that they had to left the area, so ordered the ships to reassemble and they retired at speed. Later as they rushed to the east, the first few rays of sunlight appeared in front of them, Lee knew he should have left earlier. They were restricted to *Calcutta's* speed of 28 knots, and anxious eyes keep looking to the rear.

"Radar... Bridge Air Raid warning, twenty plus aircraft." Obviously, the task force's exploits had been heard, and the Germans wanted revenge. Having the better anti-aircraft batteries, the cruisers moved to the outside, which allowed the destroyers between the cruisers, to be protected.

Lookout calls, "Ju88s sir."

"Radar… Bridge further twenty aircraft approaching"

"Stukas!" Oh my God!

"Signal the others to take independent action and movement."

'X' and 'Y' turret opened fire at maximum range, salvo after salvo as the range came down. One aircraft was hit and retired, but the others droned on.

The four-inch batteries now took up the challenge, this was *Calcutta's* forté, and her crews worked on ruthlessly, shell after shell headed skyward, then it was the close-range weapons turn. The noise was terrific. Once again, the six-inch battery opened fire on the Stukas as they approached.

Above the ships, they lined up and awaited their turn to pitch down and attack, the first group attacked *Calcutta*, the next onto *Preston*, twisting and turning they emerged from huge water spouts made by the bombs. Yet again the Stukas dived on the cruisers, more evasive manoeuvres, again *Calcutta* was hit, one medium-sized bomb landed just in front of 'A' gun, the second hit the pom-pom platform abaft the funnel, causing the 2pdr ammunition to start exploding. Another exploded to port, and her side was peppered by shrapnel. But still, she raced on, Lee watched, as her crew went about their business of engaging the enemy, and firefighting. *Hereward* was straddled by three bombs, which caused her steering gear to break down, she cut across *Preston's* bow, mercifully missing, and proceeded to do two full circuits before they were able to bring her under control. Now she was some distance away and desperately trying to catch up, her puny anti-aircraft guns trying to swat away her tormentors.

The lookouts called in unison, "Torpedo bombers approaching portside."

Lee yelled, "Where did they come from?" Four He111 torpedo bombers flew low, released together, as *Preston*, *Calcutta* and *Hotspur* turned to comb the torpedo tracks. With their loads gone the bombers lifted for the sky. This was the moment that the gunners had been waiting for, everybody with a weapon opened fire, two He 111 crashed and a third flew off, leaving a trail of black smoke.

South, they hurried, *Hereward* closing rapidly. The surviving Germans aircraft left the scene.

"Air Raid warning, 10 plus approaching from the north." Weary gun crews dragged themselves back to the weapons. Italian SM 79s high level bombers droned in, Lee watched in fascination as their bomb bay doors opened and the bombs fell away, the air around the aircraft alive with black exploding shells. This was the Italian 'B' team, as the bombs landed harmlessly astern, and one aircraft was seen to crash.

South, they kept going, the miles passing, the ship stood down from action stations, and the crew could go about their business. Soon a message was passed to the Captain, "*Preston* and *Hotspur* to return to Crete for another attack, *Calcutta* and *Hereward* to continue to Alex for repairs."

They returned the way they came, joining forces with *Ajax* (The hero of the River Plate action), *Diamond* and *Greyhound*. *Ajax* took command, and they repeated the track that *Preston* took last night. This night just a few Caiques were found and swiftly dispatched, leaving more Mountain Troops struggling in the water. On this occasion, they left at 0200 and were well south of the island by daybreak. A very pleasant sight appeared before the, a pair of long-range Beaufighter aircraft to escort them home.

Chapter 8

Having survived two, high-level bombing attacks on the way north, they arrived of the small port of Lampi. It was too shallow for *Ajax* and *Preston* to enter so the destroyers were sent in to ferry the troops out to the ships. This of course will take a lot longer to achieve. By daybreak, they were only half loaded, and the Captain of *Ajax* ordered that they remain until loaded. Lee thought this was a stupid idea, he knew what would be coming their way soon!

Hotspur came alongside, with another load of soldiers and airmen, "Come on you men hurry up!" shouted Matley, the tension was getting to everybody.

Somehow, they had not been spotted yet, but on the horizon, they could see aircraft attacking some warships. Our turn next, thought Lee. *Greyhound* came alongside with a thump, some strained rivets to be replaced, thought Lee, as he looked down at the bridge of *Greyhound*, he could see the crew were exhausted. The young Captain yelled up his apology, he looked grey with fatigue, Lee nodded, I guess I looked the same to him he thought. Finally, that's the last, so they got underway, *Greyhound* and *Hotspur* staying back to load more men. Lee was also not happy about that and signalled to *Ajax* to give them time to load and get out. The reply was curt "No." South again to Alex.

Oberleutnant Hans Müller sat at the mess table, and looked around at the empty seats. He was the commanding officer of a staffel of Ju 87 Stuka divebombers as part of Fliegerkorps X. This small airfield in Southern Greece had been his home for the past three weeks. They arrived, sixteen aircraft strong, and his men were full of optimism, after all, they had terrorized the Tommies in Norway, destroying their ships and equipment. Now they were doing the same in the Mediterranean, but what a cost. His staffel had been decimated, he was down to six serviceable aircraft, with no spare parts or tools. His 'black men' were doing miracles to keep him flying. They were also short of bombs, so they were improvising bombs from captured Greek eight-inch shells and adding crude stabilising fins to them. The crews were tired, they were awoken before daylight, they flew, bombed, returned to base, reloaded and got out again. Until dusk stopped them, then fell into their bunks and slept till they were awoken again. Why didn't these Britishers give up! Why did they keep fighting, don't they know they were beaten?

He looked at the paperwork to be completed, even now the Headquarters still wanted lists returned. The buff-coloured envelope was on the top of the pile, from the Kriegsmarine Personnel Department, notifying that his brother Eric was missing, his submarine U97 had not returned from patrol, and was presumed lost. Oh Eric, I will miss you, you so loved your job in the Navy, and were so happy when you got command of a brand-new submarine. A friend told him what they thought happened, but nothing official had been passed down.

Finally loaded *Greyhound* and *Hotspur* increased speed and hurried after the disappearing cruisers. Grossly overloaded, they had become very unstable. Both Captains hoped they would not have to take evasive manoeuvres.

Preston's Radar was watching the progress of the two destroyers as they tried to catch up, relaying information to the bridge. Lee was worried and signalled *Ajax* to slow down, so the distance could shorten between the two groups of ships. Again, a negative answer was received. Waiting a few moments, he called, "Bunts, contact *Ajax*, tell them we will have to slow down as we have an issue with the boiler feed water."

Everyone on the bridge looked around, they didn't remember hearing anything about the boilers. Lee picked up the phone, "Chief, I notice that you have a feed water problem, please make sure you put it in your deck log."

After a moment's silence the Chief grasped what was going on, "About fifteen minutes be enough, sir?"

"Well done, Chief. OOW make a note in the log, water feed problems, and log the time."

Looking around the bridge, everybody had realised what was going on and were smiling.

Hotspur and *Greyhound* had caught up, and were now huddle around *Preston*, her high-angle battery would give them some protection. *Ajax* was not happy, so no doubt Lee would hear more about it, back at base.

Overhead the shadowing aircraft was back, not long now. *Preston* and her destroyers joined up with *Ajax*, and they increased speed for Alexandria.

"Air raid, multiple aircraft from the north east." The gun crews stand too.

The first wave was Ju 87s and Ju88s. They start their attack as before, circling above then diving down. Again, the noise was terrific, the scream of aero engines, crash and bang of guns firing and the explosion of bombs. Both *Ajax* and *Diamond* were straddled, taking casualties amongst the soldiers. At last, the enemy aircraft departed. Time to bring up fresh stocks of ammunition and clear away the spent shell cases. The cooks scurried round the ship, handing out corn beef sandwiches and cups of tea from great big fannies. Again and again, the aircraft came back and all day long the attacks continued. The ships were peppered by near misses and shrapnel, and it's only down to good luck and excellent manoeuvring they survived any major damage. Night fell and the exhausted crews could stand down.

Lee retired to his sea cabin for a few minutes, to take stock of his ship. Fuel was sufficient to reach Alex, anti-aircraft ammunition was down to 25%, food and fresh water was nearly gone, and his men were exhausted, he wondered how they would cope with another day like today.

Dawn brought a force 4 sea, and clear skies, the ships rolled badly, but the radar sets showed the sky clear of aircraft. They continued, this gave his crew time to eat and clean up, the army lads offered to stand watch so his crew could go about their business. They were lucky — no further attacks — and they reached Alexandria next day at dusk. The line of trucks waiting to take off the soldiers, ammunition and fuel lighters came alongside, followed by the victualing barge. The ship was a hive of activity.

"Sir, signal from the Flag Ship, it reads Captain and Chief Engineer to report onboard at 1200 with deck logs."

"Very good."

At 1200 prompt, they set foot on the quarter-deck of *Warspite*. They were greeted by the side party and the Admiral's Flag Lieutenant. Also, at the gangway was Hughes, the Captain of *Ajax*, waiting for his launch to collect him. So, it was obvious what the meeting was about. Hughes was a very unpopular officer, but Lee treated him with the utmost courtesy.

ABC asked Lee to discuss the last operation, detail by detail. Then asked about the water feed problem. Jonesy gave a very eloquent discussion of the problem. They were then ushered into the officers' mess, and was delighted to see the Captains of the four destroyers also in there. All gathered round, shaking hands, and discussing the past few days. The Captains of *Hotspur* and *Greyhound*, shook his hand profusely and thanked him for waiting for them. The other Captains explained that they had asked Hughes to wait for the destroyers to close up, but he would not. They chatted for an hour or so, while taking coffee and sandwiches. Soon they were all summoned to see the Admiral.

"Sit down gentlemen," ABC smiled. "First of all, Captain Hughes has been relieved of his command. Lt Cdr Jackson, [Diamond's Captain] you are to take command of *Ajax*, your Number 1, will assume the role of Captain. The rest of you well done. Lee, you are to be recommended for your actions during the evacuation, I have no doubt that your actions saved the two destroyers *Hotspur* and *Greyhound* from destruction and the loss of countless lives." Everybody smiled and shook hands.

"Alan, see me after the meeting. Right, that's out of the way, what recommendations do you have for me?" The discussion was about the lack of fighter protection, carrying more AA ammunition, extra supplies of food and water and additional medical personnel, also the need for more high-angle anti-aircraft guns and AA Cruisers.

"I can't promise anything but I will see what I can do."

The meeting was finished, and they all trooped out.

"Thanks, Alan, for staying. First, that idiot Hughes was dead wrong, you were right to insist on protecting those destroyers. I have seen the signal logs, and I have a damn good idea what you were up against. How could the Captain of one of His Majesty's warships left his comrades in the lurch, it beggars belief." ABC was clearly worked up about this. "I have recommended you for a gong, you and your Chief Engineer. I don't know if it will be approved, Hughes has some powerful friends in the Admiralty. I am sorry but you will have to sail again tonight, things were desperate in Crete. Just to let you know that General Wavell was in here earlier, he was worried about the losses the Navy was taking to bring back his troops. I told him it takes three years to build a ship, it takes three centuries to build a tradition. So be off with you, and good luck." With that, Lee was dismissed.

Later, he was standing on *Preston*'s deck as *Warspite*, *Barham*, *Ajax*, *Orion*, *Fiji* and *Gloucester* with seven destroyers, left harbour. They were also en route to help with the evacuation. It took longer than expected to load the supplies. His men were exhausted. Finally, *Preston* was ready, and along with *Hotspur* and *Hereward*, made ready for sea.

Chapter 9

Again, the tannoy urged, "Special sea duty men close up, hands for leaving harbour." Yet more groans and grumbles from the crew. As they headed into the Narrows, they faced a clear starlit night, the moon high above — a hunter's moon, not what Lee wanted to see. Sitting in his chair, Timmins had brought him a cup of pusser's kye, a fortified brew made of naval block chocolate, boiling water, tinned milk and demerara sugar, with a strong tot of rum, bless you Timmins. The soft hum of the engine room fans and the gentle swoosh of the sea, would normally have made it a pleasant night, but not now, they were off to war again. Their destination was the small port of Leraptra, which had a small jetty that they hoped could be used to speed up loading. As they proceeded, the radar picked up aircraft at extreme range, but not getting any closer. Watson was checking the charts he had picked up from H.Q. They were a little out of date, fifty years to be exact! He went to the chart room again to go over his calculations.

Lee spotted the worried look on Watson's face and followed him in.

"You OK, Pilot?"

"Sir, I am worried about this chart. Its showing just enough water under the keel at the jetty, but it's not been checked in years."

"Right, what do you suggest?"

"Is there any way to have it checked by somebody on scene?"

"I don't know, I will send a signal."

Hours later, the signal came back as a negative. But Lee had an idea.

"Ask our intrepid Fly Boys to come to the bridge, also the Buffer."

A few moments later, the pilot Collins, navigator, Buffer, TAG, Watson and Lee were packed into the chart room.

Lee quickly passed on his thoughts, "Launch the Walrus with the Buffer and two hands, land near the harbour, and using the Walrus' dingy do a quick survey and pass the information back to the ship. Stay there until we arrive then we will hoist you back onboard.

"Questions? No, OK then, make sure you carry firearms just in case, DON'T let the Pongos near the aircraft, understood?" all nod. "Right as soon as you can, away you go."

Thirty mins later, the familiar bang and the stench of cordite surrounded the bridge. The 'Steam Pigeon' was away. It droned off into the sky. Looking like some prehistoric animal, it climbed slowly away. They had launched further away as they wouldn't need fuel for a return trip, they could have longer on station. The pilot settled down to a long haul, at 90 knots this was no rocket ship, the navigator plotting his course and the three extra men squeezed in the rear compartment, glad to be away from the ship for a while. The telegraphists/air gunner, made some tea from the tiny galley and passed it around, lovely stuff, and on they droned.

Three hours later, Collins circled the harbour, looking down he could see thousands of soldiers and equipment packing the roads and spare land of this little port. Somebody starts shooting at them. Bloody fools, he tilted the wings so they could see the red, white and blue roundel, and fired a red very light. Thankfully the shooting stopped, but unknown to him, the aircraft had taken a few hits in the hull and port float. One of the bullets had hit Wainright, one of the seamen, and he had bled out and died. The message was passed forward to Collins, and he was furious! He came into land, and watching the wave patten, made a perfect touchdown. He taxied towards the harbour entrance. Something was wrong with his airplane, it was sluggish and wanted to keep turning to port. Looking out of the cockpit he spotted the holes in the float; the TAG came forward to tell him they were taking in water. He taxied forward to beach the aircraft. As it grounds on the sandy shore, a mob of soldiers rushed forward towards them. Fear in their eyes, he stood up in the cockpit, the navigator manned the forward machine gun, and he fired a shot overhead from his pistol to stop the stampede. This had the desired effect.

Soon an Army Major, came forward to ask what they were there for, clearly the message from *Preston*, hadn't got through. Collins repeated his orders, and asked for some engineers to help with the bullet repairs, a burial party for Wainright, the use of a small boat, (the dingy had also being punctured) an armed guard for the Walrus. Once the reasons for their arrival was understood, all Collins' requests were granted. A small boat and some rescued sailors were found to crew it and the Buffer was off to do his surveying. Wainrights' body was taken to a nearby cemetery, and a shallow grave dug. An Army Pastor was found and Collins and a small party of sailors held a short service. Collins made certain he had all the details for the skipper.

Working furiously, the Buffer and his party surveyed the area around the jetty. Inside the harbour, it was too shallow for *Preston*, but it was sufficient for the destroyers. The outside of the jetty would take the ship, but there was not a lot of water under the keel. After the burial, Collins returned to the Walrus and supervised the repairs to the aircraft. They had been very lucky, a party of RAF personnel were close by, and had carried out the repairs. *Preston* was one hour away, and the Shagbat repaired they used the Buffer's boat to drag it off the beach and moor it in the shallow water of the harbour.

Major Collins and the Walrus' navigator had been busy, organising a loading plan, they needed to get everybody onboard as quickly as possible. All heavy weapons must be destroyed and left behind, ammunition dumped and vehicles made useless. Using the wireless from the aircraft, they contacted the ship with the vital information, and the news about the lost sailor. Lee was very upset about the matelot, a needless waste.

Collins watched the coast road, down from the cliffs, the last few stragglers making their way towards the harbour. He looked out to sea, and watched the German aircraft bomb the small flotilla of ships as they made their way landward. Would they ever stop? Don't they run out of bombs? He was so frustrated he wasn't there to help.

The ship was alongside the outer jetty wall, the two destroyers on the inside wall. The Walrus had been towed around to *Preston* and hoisted aboard. Collins urged the last party of soldiers aboard *Hotspur*, "Come on, you men, we need to go!"

The tannoy on the ship booms, "Mr Collins, that's enough, get aboard it's time to depart."

With a last look around, Collins scurried up the gangway, and it was hoisted aboard, the ship slipped from the jetty and headed home again, grossly overloaded.

"Mr Collins, report to the bridge."

Back onboard and making his way to the bridge, he was struck by the cleanliness and order onboard the ship, a contrast from the squalor on shore.

"Sir, you wanted me?"

"Thanks, Ted, join me in my cabin."

"Tell me what went on, from the moment you left the ship."

The Pilot explained everything that had happened, passing over Wainright's dog tags, and the location of his body, about the RAF lads repairing the aircraft, and the spare sailors helping out. "Sir, I would like to recommend the Buff, the Nav, and air gunner for an award, they were magnificent, and without Buff we could not have loaded so quickly."

"I agree, write it up and I will forward it up the chain. I was also speaking to the Army Major and he praised you for the work you did, he was also very sorry about our shipmate."

"Huff it should not have happened! but thank you sir."

"OK, Ted, get some rest. The Fleet is further to the west and were having a torrid time of it."

Just then, "Air raid, multiple aircraft fifty miles from the North East."

"Will it ever stop?"

Oberleutnant Eric Müller strapped himself into the aircraft, his rear gunner Gunther Werner, unimaginative but dependable, grunted as he loaded the last pan of machine gun bullets. "Herr Oberleutnant this was the last can anywhere on the station."

"We will have to stay out of trouble then Gunther." He was dog tired, he had only two aircraft left, this one and the one Rudi was flying. By rights he should ground them as they both had major defects on them, but this was all he had. He also sensed that they were at the end of this conflict, the Britishers had fled from Crete and just the last few remained. The other two squadrons were attacking a major fleet on the west of the island, but his objective was a small number of ships off the port of Lerapetra.

He joined the other squadrons as they headed south, then he peeled off with some Ju88s and headed towards *Preston's* group. Müller was struggling with the controls of his dive-bomber, it was yawing from left to right, and would not fly straight and level. Just then flak started appearing around his aircraft. Damn, these Tommies were getting better at this. The faster Ju88s flew on they were going to attack at high level. Müller watched as the bomb bay doors opened and the bombs tumbled out and down. In an instant, the lead aircraft exploded, a direct hit from a flak gun. He watched in horror as the flaming wreck headed earthwards. Now it was his turn, he was high over the ships, and he picked out the largest ship, nose down, and dropped like a stone. The aircraft was struggling in the dive and was wandering as it plummeted down, he was surrounded by exploding flak shells, but kept going. Just at the moment of bomb release, his aircraft jinxed left, throwing off the aim of the deadly missile. The 500 kg bomb screamed seaward, with *Preston* in its sights, but the jink had altered the trajectory. Luckily for *Preston*, the bomb should have gone straight into the forward boiler room, but it punctured the hangar, destroying the Walrus, exiting outboard and exploding as it hit the sea, peppering the ship's side with shrapnel.

Wounding many soldiers in the process. Müller heaved on the joystick with all his strength, just clearing the wave tops, then a loud bang behind him and the smell of cordite and the intercom had gone dead. He looked in the mirror and could see Gunther slumped over his gun, there was no response from him. He barely made it back to the airfield, the Stuka collapsing on the runway, it would never fly again. The medics rushed out to the rear cockpit, but there was nothing they could do for Gunther.

"Bridge... DCT open fire when in range." The cacophony started again, six-inch, four-inch, pom-pom, 20mm, all adding to the racket. Two Ju88s tumbled from the sky, and the ship dodged their bombs, then two Ju87 dived on the ship. The first one released its bomb which penetrated the aircraft hangar and exploded outboard, with many casualties. The second Stuka, strangely did not drop a bomb but dived straight into the sea, where it erupted in a huge explosion.

"First Aid parties to the hangar, damage control to the hangar," the tannoy shouted.

To the west, the Fleet was struggling, under increasing aerial attack. *Warspite* was hit on her starboard six-inch battery deck causing many casualties, *Orion was* hit by multiple bombs which caused massive casualties amongst the soldiers, *Fiji* and *Gloucester* were sunk with heavy loss of life, having fired off all their AA ammunition, they had had to resort to firing practice shells at their tormentors. *Ajax* hit by one bomb aft, three destroyers sunk or badly damaged. The list went on.

Preston sped south, with nothing to help their consorts with, they needed to unload and come back to support them. From nowhere *Greyhound* was straddled by a string of bombs. Unspotted, a single He111, escaped to the north, its work done. The ship started to capsize, still underway, the bows being driven under by her racing screws.

"Ask *Hotspur* to stand by *Greyhound* and see if there were any survivors." Again, *Preston* circled to add her protection to *Hotspur*.

"Radar… Bridge, two surface contact closing from the south east." The ship turned to intercept as they hoved into sight, not a good time for surface action.

"*Jaguar* and *Maori* in sight."

"Very good, ask them to stand by *Greyhound*, and ask *Hotspur* to re-join us."

On arrival at Alexandria, this time no one was waiting for them, so the survivors made their own way ashore. The ship's company started to clear away the mess left onboard. The wreckage of the Walrus was discharged onto the quay, while the engine room staff made some patches for the holes in the ship's side. There was a distinct lack of dockyard workers around. Once clear of the soldiers, the ship sailed for the duty oiler, topping up her fuel, she had not had time to get more ammunition. So, she left without it. The Fleet was being pounded as they returned from Crete. Without orders, Lee took his ship back to sea to render what help he could. She raced north. The crews stood by their weapons. Hours later, the radar picked up the echo of aircraft circling at maximum range, clearly the position of the Fleet. As she approached, a destroyer flashed a challenge, *Preston* replied immediately, it would appear that they were happy to see them. It was now dark when they finally met up. *Preston* positioned herself astern to be upthreat in the event of another air raid.

"Signal from Flag sir, nice to see you."

"Acknowledge, Bunts, no message." Lee was too tired for witty messages. They settled down to nighttime routines, the Fleet restricted to 15 knots, the speed of the damaged *Warspite*.

"Captain, Guns for you."

Lee took the phone, "Mark, what can I do for you?"

"Sir, we are short of four-inch ammunition, we are down to 35% remaining, I will have to limit the salvos we fire. Pom-pom and 20 mm are short also, and we are out, completely, of Breda ammunition."

"Thanks, for letting me know, I know you will do your best."

"Signalman pass a message to the flagship reporting our ammunition stocks."

"Aye, sir."

Dawn arrived and with it the longer-range bombers, He 111, Ju 88s and SM79s and the attack begin again. The He111 dropped low to start a torpedo attack, the Junkers approached at high-level, then started to dive bomb, and the SMs were high level bombing. A very well-coordinated attack. All the ships opened fire, and they all took independent course changes to escape the enemy attention.

The destroyer *Akron*, and the cruiser *Enterprise*, were hit by torpedoes, and they slewed out of formation. *Martin* slowed to render assistance to *Akron,* and *Hostile* turned to help *Enterprise*. *Preston* slowed down to give AA cover again. *Akron* slowly rolled over, there were very few survivors, *Martin* collected who she could. *Enterprise* was hit in the bows, but was in no danger of sinking, and with the forward bulkheads shored up, a short time later, got underway to catch up with the fleet. *Hostile* stayed with her.

That was the last air-raid on the journey back to base, and a badly battered and shaken Fleet returned to port to lick its wounds. The bulk of the army was saved, but at what cost to the Royal Navy. Three cruisers and seven destroyers sunk; multiple ships damaged. The Admiralty started an inquiry into the whole sorry enterprise, somebody needed to be made a scapegoat, so the questions began. A day after returning to harbour, two four-ring Captains and a Lt Commander, arrived at *Preston's* brow to start to question Lee. Its lasted for hours, and Lee was finally glad to see the back of them.

The ship slipped into a stupor, the crew going about its duties, like robots. The oiling, ammunition, victualing, repairs, all took longer than need be. The crew were exhausted, the queue for liberty was a very small one.

Chapter 10

Slowly after a week, the ship became alive again, the damage was made good and the ship painted from stem to stern, looking good in the sunlight. There would be no replacement Walrus, it had been decided that they would be landed from all ships of the Fleet. Which helped *Preston*, as the Dockyard staff came onboard to temporary erect more accommodation in the spare hangar. Also, the petrol tank, full of volatile fuel, was drained and converted to other uses. A proper refit was planned on her return to the UK. It was a shame as Lee liked the 'fly boys' onboard his ship, he would be sad to see them go, but experienced Fleet Air Arm crew were worth their weight in gold, so off they went back to RNAS Lee-on-Solent. Also, the shore left queues were getting longer, so 'Jack' was obviously beginning to feel better, which also brought a longer Captains defaulters table.

Ten days later, Lee got new orders. Due to the past few weeks intensive action, it would appear the *Preston*, another cruiser and a handful of destroyers were all that were combat ready, so he was to patrol along the North African coast, along with *Hotspur* and *Martin*, to try to intercept a convoy of Italian ships, heading to Benghazi with supplies. Lee summoned his senior officers. He explained what was going to happen, and checked their compartments were all OK. Nods all round, "As soon as we sail, we will carry out all the emergency drills, get everybody up to speed."

"Pilot, got all the charts you need?"

"Sir."

"Guns, are you ready?"

"Sir, all reloaded and I have scrounged a load of Breda ammo, and guns from the army. It's stored in the aft 20mm magazine."

"Well done, I had a reprimand from ABC about letting the stocks get so low, but there was no malice in it, I think he was glad to see us. OOW to get my launch ready I will call on *Hotspur* and *Martin*, and speak to them personally."

Onboard *Hotspur*, Rankin, the skipper, greeted Lee warmly, and pumped his hand heartily, "Once again I have to thank you for giving us protection, we were struggling with short range weapons, we feel so naked."

They discussed the past few weeks and the upcoming operation, then Lee had an idea. He contacted *Preston*, "I want to talk to Lt. Beddall."

"Sir."

"Mark, get in the Captain gig and come over to *Hotspur*, quick as you can."

Sat in Rankins cabin, twenty mins later, drinking a hot pot of tea, a tap at the door, a voice shouted, "Lt Beddall from *Preston*, sir."

"Enter."

"Ah Mark, were there more Bredas at that army dump you went to?" Lee asked

"Yes, sir they had quite a few, but the Army boys don't like them, personally I think they are a good gun."

"Right, with your permission, Captain Rankin, take the *Hotspur*'s gunnery officer and a few hands, go to that dump and get at least eight guns, more if you can and as much ammo as possible, then return here and assist them with the positions for mounting them, and I want you back onboard by 1900hrs."

"Will do, sir." And with a nod of approval from Rankin, Beddall was off on a mission."

"That's a good officer you have their sir, can I have him," he laughed.

Lee also laughed, "Nice try, but no chance."

At 0500 the ship left her moorings and headed for the entrance, ahead was *Hotspur* and following was *Martin*. As the sunlight improved, Lee could see *Hotspur* had sprouted a few more gun barrels. No doubt some dockyard know-all, would have a moan about them, but they were needed now. *Martin* was more modern and better equipped for anti-aircraft fire. *Hotspur* needed them, and should have had them months ago. As they left the narrows and turned west, they were about twenty-five miles from the coast.

The destroyers go to cruising stations on either side of *Preston*. Lookouts scanned the sky, and the radar eye looked further out. Action exercises had begun, with much moaning from the crew. With a gentle roll the ship shouldered her way forward. Beddall had come to Lee on the bridge to discuss *Hotspur*'s gun improvement. He was not too impressed with *Hotspur*'s gunner, he had to be coaxed into doing everything, so in the end, Mark stayed longer than he should to make sure the guns were sited properly, no wonder Rankin wanted to keep him.

He also had another problem, Sub Lt Richardson, Beddall's assistant, during the last air attack, was missing from his post, and was found in a small office in the transmitting station. Richardson stated he was checking data, but Lee did not believe him, as he was very jumpy during the last few days in action. Guns had asked the ship's Doctor to have a look at him. Another problem that had to be dealt with. Having survived the Norway campaign and the loss of his ship, he would ask Matley to talk to him.

The following day they got a surface contacts at extreme range on the radar set, to the north east. Lee knew he was the only naval force out here, so these must be Italians. Calling a senior officers' meeting, he explained that he wanted to attack at midnight so altered course to facilitate that, action stations to be called at 2300.

He watched the radar plot as the convoy came closer, four ships in two columns of two, a small escort to the west and a larger escort to the east, and another following. He ordered the destroyers to follow him in line astern, but this time *Martin* led, she had a better radar, and *Hotspur* brought up the rear. This would be a manoeuvre the destroyers had practised for years, so they knew it well. He planned to circle to the north and fire torpedoes, then open fire with the main guns, haul off and let the destroyers deal with anything left afloat.

Onboard the German Destroyer *Hermes* (ZG-3), KorvetteKaptain, Johan Rindt, looking though his binoculars at the small convoy. He did not have a high regard for the Italian Navy, they were sloppy in everything they did, look at the Italian escort *Marlin* astern, belching out smoke again. Because the Italians were short of warships, he had been sent to Brindisi to help escort this convoy of material for the Afrika Corps. They were on a rush to get to the Suez Canal, and needed these supplies.

He had lost his ship, Z19, at the second battle of Narvik, when he had run out of ammunition and fuel, and had to run the ship aground to save the crew. So, he had served some time at the Naval Headquarters, before being sent to Piraeus to take command of *Hermes*. She had been built in Britain for the Greek Navy, using the plans of a 'G' class destroyer and named *Vasilefs Georgios*. She had been captured, when the floating dry dock she was in, was sunk by Stuka Dive bombers. With little damage she was rapidly taken into German Service and renamed *Hermes*. From the little time he had been onboard, he had been impressed with the build quality and she was fast and very manoeuvrable. The flak guns were poor but some vierling guns had been found and fitted. His crew were all German naval ratings, so they knew what they were doing, but it was taking time to get used to this ship. Just another few hours to go, and he could hand over this convoy at Benghazi and head back to Taranto.

On *Preston,* "DCT… Bridge, the destroyer to the west looks like one of ours." The Director Control Tower had better optics than the bridge and could make out the target better than the bridge personnel could.

"Check fire, get a visual on that destroyer before opening fire."

"Sir."

"Chief Yeoman, send a message to Alexandria, to find out if we have any shipping in the area."

On *Hermes*, the lookout called, "Captain, I have two ships to port moving slowly north."

"Action stations, the only ships out there must be Britishers."

"Confirm targets." Soon the reports were coming in. A Town class light cruiser, and two destroyers. He was out-numbered and out-gunned, but it looked like they hadn't spotted him yet. "Signal, *Marlin* and *Acro* to join me, convoy was to scatter to the south. Still no reaction from the British."

Onboard *Preston*, Alexandria had signalled, definitely no British warships in this area. "Very well, commence the attack." Just then, *Martin* exploded with a might roar, a column of flame reached 100 foot into the air.

"Asdic, sir, high speed propellers to the west." It was too late to attack with torpedoes, so *Preston* and *Hotspur* commenced firing, the radar giving precise ranges.

Very soon the Italian warships were hit, *Marlin* and *Acro* were ablaze. The German destroyer, her torpedoes had found one target, was now laying smoke to protect her charges, as they headed to the south. *Preston* fired by radar ranging, and managed to hit two merchant ships and repeatedly straddled the *Hermes*. Zig Zagging for all he was worth *Hermes* circled round to the west, he wanted to have another go at the cruiser, but smoke was making it difficult. Yet he still kept getting straddled. Obviously, the Brits could see better than him.

Lee called off the attack, time to look for *Martin* survivors. The two smaller escorts, and one of the merchantmen had been sunk, but the others had escaped. Damn.

Collecting very few survivors, *Preston* and *Hotspur* retraced their steps to Alexandria. Approaching the narrowed, *Hotspur* got a submarine contact and turned to attack. She made multiple attacks, her frustration about the past few weeks being taken out on the submarine below her. Suddenly a submarine surfaced astern of *Hotspur*, and she slewed around to engage the sub. *Hotspurs* 'A' and 'B' gun opened fire, along with the 20mms. The conning tower and hull sparkled as the shells hit and ricocheted off the subs toughened sides.

Lee signalled, "Don't ram, see if you can capture!" The destroyer acknowledged, and turned to port, the main guns couldn't depress sufficiently to fire, so the Bredas kept firing to keep the subs crew below decks. *Preston* circled the two of them, this was not a fight for a cruiser, so she stays out of it.

Slowly the submarine started to sink by the stern, her bows rising higher in the water. She held for a moment then slid stern first into the deep, a handful of survivors left swimming in the filthy water. *Hotspur*'s launch was sent to collect them. Both ships' company started to cheer!

"Signal from *Hotspur*, sir, Italian sub, *Marco Polo*, is no more."

"Thanks, signal, *Hotspur*, well done. Pilot take us into port please, but let *Hotspur* go first, she deserves it."

At last, the Fleet had something to cheer about as *Hotspur* led *Preston* into port and was given a rapturous welcome.

Later onboard *Warspite*, Lee was in discussion with ABC and his staff about this mysterious destroyer, and why he had waited to confirm its identity and lost the element of surprise.

Fresh orders: they were to escort a small convoy from Alexandria to Haifa. This became the norm for the next few weeks, as the Admiralty tried to find sufficient ships to send to Alex to make up the losses.

On the return trip, from dropping supplies at Tobruk, the Chief came up to the bridge to see Lee. If Jonesy was up here it must be important.

"Sir we have a major problem, the Port cruising turbine has thrown a blade. It smashed the casing taking out both feed pumps. I can't do anything here, we would need a dockyard. Also the gland space had started leaking again. It's all the high speed and violent running we've been doing over the past months."

"Thanks, Eric, I will pass the message on to the Admiralty, I guess we have to shut the Turbine down?"

If the Chief could have repaired it, he would, so it was serious.

Limping back into port, and with a maximum speed of 18 knots, *Preston* was now a cripple. When they went alongside, the Dockyard manager and the Fleet Engineering Team were waiting to come aboard. They all hurried below, and a few minutes later, Admiral Cunningham came aboard.

Lee showed him around, he also wanted to meet some of the crew and have a talk to them. This was well received. After which they retired to Lee's cabin. Timmins had laid out a spread for the Admiral. "Alan, I have found out about that Eyetie destroyer from a few weeks ago. She was Greek and the Germans had captured her, and renamed her *Hermes*. Apparently, the Skipper is some hotshot destroyer driver from the

Narvik Battle. There will be an intelligence briefing sent out to everybody about it, thought I would let you know first." They sat and chatted for a while and ABC told Lee about the ships that were on the way, but the war was not going well for Britain. The Germans were pushing the 8th Army back towards Egypt and the convoys were being decimated in the Atlantic, so its tighten your belts and do your best.

The damaged engine could not be repaired here, so the ship continued running on one engine and just went on small escort missions. Within a week, the Battleship *Valiant* and three new *Dido* class cruisers have arrived, along with eight destroyers. The Mediterranean Fleet was starting to grow again. Finally, they were given their orders: proceed to Durban for dry docking, for the leaking gland space, then Portsmouth for the refit and repairs.

Chapter 11

Not needing the additional 20mm guns, they were landed to be used on other ships. Then, south down through the Suez Canal, the Red Sea. Lee was exhausted, so in these calmer and safer waters, he took the chance to rest. He also called the Doctor and the ship's Chaplin in for talks. A few days later he was rested, and the ship called at Mombasa for fuel. The underlying tension and stress for the crew, had lifted like a fog. Tired men were recovering, and people like Richardson, were seen around the ship smiling. Lee thought, I must get him transferred to a hospital, he was clearly struggling with combat, and the crew notice these things. Onwards to Durban, at 12 knots this was no speed trip.

The Buffer came to the bridge, "Permission to speak, sir."

"Yes, Buffer."

"Sir, can we have a 'crossing the line ceremony', there were a lot of lads onboard who haven't done it yet?"

Lee smiled, "What a wonderful idea, team up with the Cox'n and No. 1 and get it sorted." As they headed towards the equator, the ship was a hive of activity as a dunking pool, swimming pool and a throne for King

Neptune was constructed on the catapult deck, at the side of the aircraft crane. Costumes were made and the ship made ready for the great day.

King Neptune, aka the Pilot, arrived onboard with his entourage, some of which were quite alluring in their mermaid costumes, and the uninitiated crew members were lined up for the ceremony. His 'poly wogs' were sent around the ship to collect the recalcitrant members who were in hiding and were brought to the dunking pool. The unpopular members got a particularly heavy soaping, Richardson amongst them. After the ceremony was over, the chef and his crew, organised a BBQ to round off a great day. Tomorrow, there would be a few sore heads and bruises around.

They arrived in Durban and anchored in the harbour, the cruiser *Kenya* was still in the drydock and they had to wait till next day to replace her. The crew were eager to get ashore. All the older hands spread stories about the exotic African ports. Around late afternoon, *Kenya* was floated out. *Preston* took her place in the drydock. Unfortunately, for the crew it was a short visit, the ship was refloated the next day, the leak now fixed. But just enough time for the crew to have a short run ashore and buy more trinkets. Then they continued their journey home.

Round the Cape, they headed straight into a storm, which battered the ship for three days, and then they received a message from the Admiralty, to swing past the island of Tristan De Cunha, to check everything was

OK. Once past the island, they again headed north, contacting Jamestown, the capitol of Tristan, as they passed, all in order.

200 miles north, the Radar Office reported two surface contacts ahead, at maximum range.

Out here, we were way off the shipping lanes, thought Lee. He ordered a course to intercept them. As the range dropped, Lee had an uneasy feeling about this, so ordered the ship to action stations. The two merchant ships appeared over the horizon, and they were very close together, that was strange.

"Signalman, ask them to identify themselves. Then contact the Admiralty and tell them what's going on." As the range shortened, the merchant ships, rapidly diverged and were increasing speed.

"The one to port says she is the *Paris*, from Portugal, and the other, *Waterhen*, from Greece," the signal man called.

Lee ordered, "Mr Vickers, check the movements log, see if they are genuine." They were rapidly increasing the distance between themselves. "Pilot, what do you make of them?" Being ex-Merchant Navy, he would have better knowledge.

"Sir, they are not listed on the movements log, and there is something not right about them, they look strange!" Watson replied.

"Bunts, tell them to heave too, and await inspection."

They were slowing down, and both turning onto a northern heading. *Preston* turned to pass the port side of *Waterhen*, "Sir, why don't we go between them!" asked one of the midshipmen.

"I don't want to be caught with them on either side of me until I know they were genuine," replied Lee.

They were close to *Waterhen*, the DCT and the main battery slowly turning to keep a lock on the ship. Ahead of them, *Paris* turns slightly, and Watson said, "What's he doing?" Two things happened at once, screens on the ship's side fell away, and a large packing crate on the deck changed into a gun mounting, and the German ensign broke from *Paris'* mainmast. Lee was caught slightly off guard; he had been watching *Waterhen*. The first salvo from the *Paris* straddled *Preston*, with two hits in the forward crew mess deck. Then *Waterhen* did the same act, the ships sides dropped away and four guns opened fire. Beddall, fortunately, was on the ball, and ordered open fire without Lee's permission. At pointblank range, all eight, six-inch shells smashed into *Waterhen*, but she had also hit *Preston*, one shell hitting the after P2 mounting and the other hit just below the quarterdeck, where it smashed into the Officers mess. The *Paris* had found the range and hit *Preston* on the aft funnel and the aircraft hangar. Beddall changed from armour-piercing, to high-explosive shells, and gave the *Waterhen* another full broadside, which tore the ship apart, then shifted target to *Paris*, the first salvo going over. Being unable to increase speed, *Preston* turned to use *Waterhen* as a shield, while firing at *Paris*. Beddall, used 'A' 'B' turrets to fire another salvo at *Waterhen* and 'X' 'Y at *Paris*.

But *Waterhen* was not finished, a wounded Petty Officer, staggered to the torpedo tubes and had managed to train the twin tubes at *Preston* and fired. The first torpedo failed to launch, but the second ran straight and true, and scored a hit on the bows of *Preston*. She shuddered with the impact of the torpedo; a huge column of water rose at the bow. Now *Preston* had to stop firing 'A' gun, the damage was causing flooding in the forward magazine but she was in a rhythm and repeatedly hit *Paris*, who managed to get another hit on *Preston*, but this was on 'B' boiler room, which caused great damage and casualties.

It was a short but vicious fight, with both merchantmen eventually sinking and *Preston* badly damaged.

Lee ordered a cease fire and the surgeon and his staff started treating casualties, and the Chief checked on the damage. The hit on P2 mounting had also damaged the majority of the ship's boats. As only the launch was available, that was sent to pick up survivors.

Lee remembered the trick with the last prisoners onboard, and put them in a mess deck and got his German speakers to listen in on the conversations.

Preston was badly damaged, but the bulkheads were holding, they have three dead and twenty-five injured, and had collected forty-three survivors from both ships. The Chief, Buffer, and his crew were working miracles, the boiler room was now water tight, but too badly damaged to be used. The P2 mounting was wrecked along with two of the 20mm gun tubs.

At 12 knots, they head for Freetown. The ship slowly made progress, but she rolled badly in the quarter sea.

Freetown, what a dump! It had no redeeming features, just an oiler and a store ship to meet the needs of the Fleet. The mosquitos must have heard that fresh blood was onboard *Preston*, and they tormented the crew mercilessly. More repairs could be carried out while at anchor. The prisoners were landed. Lee was glad to get rid of them, what a surly lot, all Kriegsmarine regulars. 'The listeners', had managed to find out that these were two AMC/Raiders that had been sinking ships in the Atlantic and Indian Oceans, *Paris* had been returning to Germany for leave and repairs, and was passing parts and ammo to *Waterhen*, to replace her stocks. The Admiralty knew nothing about these two, so a coup for Lee.

She continued with her journey home, still at 12 knots. They were near the Cape Verde Islands when two destroyers rendezvoused with them, and escorted them to Cape Trafalgar. Here two more destroyers replaced the first two, and they continued north. The Admiralty were taking no chances, they wanted *Preston* home safe. Nearing Land's End, three sloops joined the little convoy, and they proceeded towards the Channel and Pompey!

Chapter 12

After discussing the needs of the ship, the bulk of the crew went on left. *Preston*, entered Number 5 drydock. There she had her bows temporarily plated over and made watertight. 'A' turret lifted out and the gun ring covered over. The destroyed four-inch gun mounting was removed and landed. The many shrapnel holes were patched up and the hull made watertight. The damaged engine was disconnected from the prop shaft, ready for her trip across the Atlantic.

Eight days later, *Preston* was floated out of the dock. Engine parts and other equipment were loaded onboard, ready for the US dockyard when needed.

Lee was surprised to see the bulk of the crew were dispatched to other duties, promotions, training etc. All he had was a steaming party. So, he could not fight or run away, as there were insufficient crew onboard. He raised this with the Admiralty manning department. They explained that with the growing needs of the Fleet, trained sailors were in short supply. So, having a fully combat-ready crew sat in America for six months was not acceptable.

His orders were to sail to Liverpool, there he was to join an outbound convoy to Halifax NS, then down the US coast to New York for refit and repair.

Following the minesweepers out of Portsmouth and into the Solent, *Proud Preston* started her journey north. With the missing 'A' turret, the ship was lighter in the bows, and needed more rudder movement to stay on course, and at 12 knots it seemed very slow. Three anti-submarine trawlers joined, and escorted her down The Channel to Lands' end, then up the Irish Sea to Liverpool.

At Liverpool, *Preston* had to go into Cammell Lairds yard on the Wirral, that gland space was leaking again. Soon undocked, she moved back into the Mersey and awaited the assembly of the convoy she was about to join.

The phone rang in Lee's day cabin, "OOD sir, launch approaching, with the convoy escort commander onboard." "Very good, I will come up," replied Lee.

Grabbing his cap, and a moment later, Lee was standing on the quarterdeck watching the launch approach. A very smart crew of WRENs went through their evolutions as she slowed, then stopped at *Preston*'s gangway. From beneath a Commander's hat complete with scrambled egg on the peak, a broad-smiling Gil Nunn saluted the quarterdeck.

After lunch, the two old friends were discussing the Atlantic trip ahead. Lee was very happy to see his old No. 1. They chatted and reminisced until early evening when Nunn received a message to return to his ship, but they arranged for Lee to go onboard Nunn's ship, *Pimpernel,* the following forenoon. What crew remained were granted left to visit the hotspots of Liverpool, but being berthed in the river there were few takers.

As Lee approached the *Pimpernel*, this was the first time he has been able to study these tiny 'Jack of all Trades'. Her sides were badly rusted and salt encrusted, but the moment he stepped abord, he could tell this was a top-notch warship. Everything was in good order and well maintained, the crew looked smart and efficient, a credit to her captain. Nunn then proceeded to give Lee the full guided tour of his command. After twelve months in command, and two German submarines to his credit, Nunn had been given command of the 23rd Escort Group. This sounded grand, but consisted of three Flower-class Corvettes, his own *Pimpernel*, *Rose*, and *Fennel*, and two coal-burning anti-submarine trawlers, *Oak* and *Tapdancer*. But for Nunn he was so proud that they could have been a squadron of battle cruisers. Their first task as a group was to safely escort this thirty-six-ship convoy and *Preston*, to the USA.

They started to left the Mersey estuary, the corvettes leaving first to check for any subs lurking around the entrance, then the merchant ships, followed by the trawlers then *Preston*. The trawlers then started ushering the ships into their convoy positions, with *Preston* in the very centre of the convoy, with the three corvettes across the front of the convoy box and the trawlers brought up the rear. Nunn had explained that being coal fired they were really critical on fuel consumption and needed to be conserved, so only used them as rescue ships. Lee had proposed that *Preston* would tow, first *Oak* for three days, then *Tapdancer* for three days. That would extend their range by a considerable amount. When the convoy box was ready and underway, *Oak* came astern of *Preston* and the tow commenced, being all ex-trawler men, this evolution was carried out very smartly, then this changed to *Tapdancer* three days later, this also being done promptly.

As they cruised west, into a head sea, at a steady pace of 6 knots, (this speed was governed by the slowest ship in the convoy, *Talybont*, an old tramp steamer built in 1891, and still afloat!) it seemed like they would never get to America. As they went around the top of Ireland and into the Atlantic proper, they became aware of a FW 200 Condor aircraft shadowing the convoy. The Condor pilot, once he was happy, and knew that this convoy was heading west and contained a cruiser, passed this information on to headquarters in France. Then turned to drop his bomb load on the convoy. These landed about three columns over and caused no damage. Satisfied with his days' work, he then returned to his base, also in France. Lee was hoping to have a crack at the Condor, but could only assemble one-gun crew, so let it be. The seas started to rise and the barometer started to drop, they were in for a blow!

The storm fell across the convoy a few hours later, with howling winds, torrential rains, and waves over fifteen feet in height. The empty cargo ships soon became scattered by the wind and tide action. At 10,000 tons *Preston* was struggling, but the diminutive corvettes and trawlers were taking it badly. Lee had safety lines rigged, and banned all access to the upper deck. The sea was taking its toll on the ship, life rafts, boats, lockers guardrails etc. were all washed away. The patches in the bow and boiler room were starting to leak, and the Chief was worried about pumping out the water with the ship being shorthanded. At one stage, Lee had to turn the ship into the wind, to take the pressure off the forward bulkhead. Everywhere he looked the convoy had disappeared it was as if *Preston* was sailing all alone. The radar was showing ships in the vicinity, but none were in view. For two days the storm tormented the ships of the convoy.

Dawn on the fourth day found *Preston* proceeding west, but the seas and wind had subsided, and the battered and tired crew members could start making repairs. Looking from the bridge, a handful of ships were in view. *Pimpernel* started signalling, could *Preston's* radar help to round up the convoy. This started a twelve-hour search for missing stragglers. In groups of threes and fours the ships came back, the three corvettes chasing round chivvying up the cargo ships into some sort of order. There were six ships missing and more worryingly *Tapdancer* was absent. Smoke on the horizon announced the arrival of *Oak*, but no sign of *Tapdancer*. Nunn ordered *Rose*, to make a sweep astern to see if they could spot the missing trawler. *Tapdancer* was not answering her radio and there was no trace of her at fifty miles out. The resurrected convoy proceeded on its way west. The following morning *Rose* hove in sight, her signal light sending a long message to Nunn, but read by *Preston's* signalmen. "Some debris and a lifebelt spotted with *Tapdancer*'s name on it, also personal items and ship's documents. Presumed ship lost."

Poor *Tapdancer* lost at the height of the storm, with nobody aware of her passing. What a cruel way to go. It was a very sombre time on all of the convoy escorts. The padre held a short ceremony for the missing on the Quarterdeck, but the attendance was low. The convoy settled back into its routine, still plodding on to America.

"Captain, sir, message from the Admiralty to *Pimpernel*, repeated for us. It reads 'suspected two U-boats ahead, consider changing course."

Moments later, signal from C.O. 23 E.G., 'Alter course due south for eight hours then back to original course. Commence zig-zag.' On, they plod still at a stately 6 knots.

A few hours later, "Radar... Bridge intermittent echo at 50 miles due north."

"Very good, pass the message on to the Captain, and also pass to *Pimpernel*."

Lee was sat in his chair checking Mr. Vickers' journal. "Sir, why did we change course to the South?"

the midshipman asked. Lee liked Vickers; he thought he would make a good officer one day.

"By heading south, we will avoid being spotted by the U-boat, we will have put about seventy-two miles between us and them, a U-boat has only a limited horizon from there conning tower, so hopefully they will not see us, and we don't want to go too far south, otherwise we will have a longer trip to Halifax," replied Lee.

Vickers looked thoughtful, "Thanks sir."

After eight hours, the convoy turned north west towards Halifax, night had descended, and all the ships settled down to night cruising stations. In his sea cabin, Lee turned restlessly in his bunk, something was not right, he had had this feeling for a few hours now. He got up and dressed in his sea-going gear, making a cup of coffee from his pantry and headed the few paces to the bridge. He found Watson on the bridge, "Evening Pilot, all quiet?"

"Yes, sir, but I don't like this full moon, makes us stand out, if I was back in civvy street I would enjoy this evening, but not now."

"I know what you mean." They chatted for a while; then Lee decided to take a turn around the ship before going back to his bunk. With so few crew onboard it was difficult to find anyone awake who were not on duty. He headed for the radar and radio offices, and stopped for a chat, to see what the crew were grumbling about. He was just passing though the watertight door to the main deck, when the door slammed backwards into him with considerable force. Then a loud explosion and a pressure wave assault him.

He woke up, covered in dust and the pungent smell of burning, the alarm rattlers were screaming, 'Action Stations' and a Radar Operator was kneeling next to him, helping him get up.

"You OK, sir?"

"Yes, yes, help me to the bridge, Smallman."

He arrived on the bridge, but he was in pain from his ribs, he was certain that one or more were broken. "Pilot, what's happened?"

"The tanker abeam us, the *Hudson Deep*, has been torpedoed. Being empty but full of petrol fumes, she has disintegrated. But we were the nearest ship so we have taken the bulk of the blast. I have damage control going round the ship now checking on damage. Also a freighter astern of us, *Manchester Trader*, has been hit and *Oak* was standing by her. Sir, you were bleeding! Come and sit in your chair. First Aid party to the bridge, Captain has been injured."

"Message from *Fennell*, am attacking, U-boat on the surface starboard side. *Rose* has been ordered to join her."

"Message from *Oak,* am picking up survivors from *Hudson Deep*." Unbelievably, some had survived.

The bridge phone rings, "Chief here sir, we have taken a lot of blast damage, but apart from a few small leaks forward, we were watertight and the engine was OK."

"Thanks Eric."

The hunt for the U-boat went on for hours with no result, the convoy increased speed, and moved further away, *Fennell* and *Rose* were recalled. *Oak* stayed with the damaged cargo ship, whose crew had managed to get her underway again, and were slowly catching up from astern. The attack had obviously made an impression on *Talybont*, who came sprinting through the convoy at speed, with sparks and black smoke belching from her spindly funnel.

Lee was in his bridge cabin, with the S.B.A., having his ribs attended too. Having had the ship's doctor, reassigned to another ship, he had to make do with a Sick Berth Attendant, who had done his best. As he was leaving, he turned to Lee, "Sir, you should rest in your cabin till we get to Canada, your ribs need time to heal."

"Thanks, I will see what I can do." They both knew that Lee would soon be back on the bridge.

There were no more scares, and they made landfall at Halifax Nova Scotia, and entering the naval dockyard, with the imposing fortress of Halifax Citadel, overlooking the bay. Tugs eased *Preston* against the Purdy's Wharf Jetty. An ambulance was waiting for the injured to be taken to hospital. Nunn had radioed ahead and arranged for Lee to be taken to the Halifax Infirmary, much to Lee's annoyance.

Chapter 13

Watson was too junior to be allowed to take *Preston* to New York, so a spare Captain was found to do the trip, Lee being confined to bed for a few weeks. Lying in a fresh clean bed, that wasn't moving, platefuls of fresh food, pretty nurses coming to see a war hero, and very efficient doctors — what luxury! All too soon he was ready to leave hospital, back to reality, and re-join his ship.

Somehow Timmins had arranged for a fresh uniform and cap, to be ready for his departure. So, dressing gingerly, he looked in the mirror, he was shocked to see his hair had turned grey literally overnight. Making his thanks to all the doctors and nurses, he made his way outside, where a huge gleaming Buick saloon car and driver was waiting. First call, the Port Admiral, so off they went to Admiralty House. Here he was greeted by the Commander in Chief of the Canadian Navy, who welcomed him warmly and had a light-hearted talk about his time in the Mediterranean and the future of the Navy. After which he was escorted back to his car and driver, who took him to Halifax train station, where he started his journey south to re-join his ship.

A long intermittent trip to New York, took two days, although seated in first-class, he had his own steward to look after him. Lee was surprised at the opulence of the 'New World', all the shops full of goods, car dealerships packed with new cars, bright lights everywhere — after the blackout in Britain, it took some getting used to. Then a taxi ride from Grand Central Station to the HQ of the Royal Navy detachment at the Brooklyn Navy Yard, where he reported for duty.

The Royal Navy building had been a very grand hotel, requisitioned for the war. Here Lee was given a room on the top floor, with a view over the East River, and if he stood in the very far side of the window, he could just make out *Preston*. As he was shown to his room by a very pretty WREN, she explained that Commanding Officers got the top floor, ratings got the lower floors and officers in-between, which made Lee smile. The restaurant was on the ground floor. Lee was weary after his travel, so went to bed early, where he fell fast asleep.

The following morning, after breakfast, his instructions were to report to the dock office. He made his way to *Preston*, which was high and dry in No. 3 dry dock. The change after just a few weeks was remarkable. The ship was covered in scaffolding, tarpaulins and very noisy dockworkers, who appeared to like making lots of noise. The scene could have been any dockyard in the world, rivet hammers pounding away, welding lighting up metalwork, and gallons of red lead paint. The bow had been removed and a new one was in the process of being fitted. The engine and boiler rooms were open to the elements and the whole world could see her scars. He stood for a few moments taking in the sights and sounds. Walking along the drydock, he spotted a sign on an office door which read 'HMS Preston only, all others stay out'. So, he had found the dock office, he smiled to himself. He was just about to open the door, when three huge dockworkers came out, two smoking huge cigars and the other chewing gum, "Sorry, Mac," said the one chewing, as they continued on their way, loaded up with blueprints and notebooks.

Entering the office, Lee was pleased to see Jonesy and Vickers, sat at a table drinking coffee. They were all very glad to see each other, and spent half an hour catching up. Jonesy then told Lee about the trip down from Halifax, under the standby skipper. On leaving her berth in Halifax, he had managed to collide with the Halifax to Dartmouth ferry. He had also insisted on running the remaining engine, despite Jonesy's warnings, at full power. This caused the turbine to fail just as they entered the East River, and had to ask for tug assistance. Apparently, the Yanks weren't impressed. As soon as they docked, he jumped in a taxi and left, Watson was left to deal with everything else. He then explained that there was a spare set of turbine blades here in New York, that had been sent in anticipation of *Gloucester's* refit, also some of the spares that they had brought with them had been damaged in the *Hudson Deep* explosion, so again they were using *Gloucester* parts. *Gloucester* had been sunk in the Med a few months before, so her parts were available. The refit was ahead of schedule, and they could not believe how fast the American workers progressed, nothing was too much trouble for them. There was also many 'extras' that were not on the list, that had also been fitted. Some fittings were a great idea, the ice cream dispensers and Coca Cola fountains, extra lockers for the crew, and canteens instead of mess deck catering. The 20mm and pom-pom mountings were being fitted with heaters, that would help the gun crews on cold days, good ideas. However, the new washrooms, with bench seat arrangement and no cubicles were not well received, and were in the process of being changed back to normal 'Heads'.

It had been agreed amongst the officers, that all the crew should take three weeks leave in turn; hence the reason Watson was not there. The ship had been adopted by the residents of New Jersey, and all the crew were allocated to an American family. They came and took them into their homes, gave the matelots, money, (ratings pay did not go far in the land of plenty), took them to the theatre etc. and many lost their hearts to these lovely people. Lee was very lucky, his family were Mr. and Mrs. Bill Crean, the descendants of an Irish emigrant family. Bill was a retired Army Air Force technician and Lee was delighted to swap stories with him. They stayed in touch well after the war ended. As the other officers took their leave, Lee was happy to take up the slack at the dock office during the day, and visits to the Creans in the evening. To be fair the Dockyard staff, knew what they were doing and, on the whole, left him alone.

When it was his leave, he decided that he needed some time travelling and Lee took himself on a train journey. So, the Crean's dropped him off at Grand Central, and he bought an Amtrac rover ticket. There he travelled down to Washington, Norfolk, then Charlestown, where he had a few days' rest. From there he went to Atlanta, Dallas, El Paso, and San Diego. After a brief stop, he travelled on to Los Angeles, San Francisco, across the Rockies to Denver, Chicago, and finally back to New York. Everywhere he went, and once they realised he was a British Naval Officer, he was met with the same kindness and friendship that the Creans had shown him.

All too soon, he was back at the dock office, *Preston* had been refloated and towed across the dock to have her final fitting-out undertaken. She looked splendid, her new bow and engine room armour replaced, and resplendent in a new camouflage coat of paint. New radar sprung up on the DCT and foremast, HF/DF mast on the rear superstructure, more life rafts, and the aircraft hangar converted properly to accommodate a cinema. The temporary mess decks added in Egypt (seemed like a lifetime ago, thought Lee) made permanent. The single 20mm guns had been replaced with twin 20mm and two additional mountings added, the pom-poms remained the same, but three twin 40mm Bofors guns had been added to the hanger roof and rear superstructure. A Talk Between Ships (TBS) system had been installed, that would help in the coming months, but only if other ships were fitted with it.

All too soon it was time to leave, they had spent the past week doing trials, full power runs, and adjustments and correcting faults. The additional draft of crewmen had arrived, she would collect the rest back at Plymouth along with her missing 'A' turret and P2 mounting. It was time to say goodbye, so like at Swan Hunters, the ship's company holds a children's party for the workers families. This went down a storm, with many happy and smiling faces.

The crew mustered, ready for departure, but three crewmen were missing, tempted by this lovely country. As deserters, if caught they would receive severe punishment by the authorities. The FBI were very good at catching these men, so Lee knew what was awaiting them. Three tugs mustered along *Preston's* sides, they took the strain and moved her into the East River, where they turned her, bows downriver and cast off. The ship gave three blasts on her foghorn as a 'thank you', and slowly moved downstream. Under the Williamsburg, Manhattan, and Brooklyn Bridges, she moved on, the crowds thronged to the river banks to wish the ship a safe journey. Past Governor's Island and the Statue of Liberty, she then increased speed and entered the

Atlantic, America and the rest times were over, it was back to wartime Britain and the blackout.

Preston met up with the cruiser *Phoebe*, which had been extensively rebuilt in the Norfolk shipyards, and like *Preston* was returning to the UK, where she would complete repairs and man the ship. They settled down to a steady 20 knots as they progressed homewards. The sea was kinder than the trip out, and they make good time.

"Radar... Bridge, small surface echo ahead about twenty miles, possible U-boat, sir."

OOW asked, "Course and speed of target."

"Captain to the Bridge, action stations."

The Alarm rattlers screamed 'Action Stations'.

Lee was on the bridge, in a flash, "Masthead lookout, what can you see?"

"Nothing yet, sir," came the reply.

"Radar why have we only just seen it?"

"It's a very small echo, sir, and we are certain it's not under power."

Slowly the ship caught up with the target. "Masthead, sir, it's a ships boat, looks like people onboard."

"Very good, tell the Buffer to take it port-side waist." As they got close, they could see people lolling around the tiller and oars. Lee watched from the bridge wing, as the ship slowed to allow the boat to come alongside. Nobody moved on the boat, so a seaman was sent aboard to help. He knelt down by the man on the tiller, then suddenly jumped back, turned and vomited over the side. The boat's crew had been dead for a very long time, seabirds had pecked out the eyes of the dead, and the flesh was falling from their bones.

"Oh God," said Lee. "Buff, see if can find any papers or documents, and ask the Padre to say a few words, then let them go."

Thirty minutes later they were underway, the lifeboat slipped fast astern, the lifeboat was from the steamship, *Vesuvius*, lost by U-boat attack nine weeks ago. The first officer, bosun and eight men made it safely to the lifeboat, but had since perished. God rest their souls.

As they approached the English Channel, *Phoebe* said her goodbyes, and headed for Portsmouth, while *Preston* made for Plymouth. Very soon she was tied up again at the South Yard Wall. The missing guns were on the dockside awaiting fitment. Extra equipment was also to be loaded, and the remainder of her crew would join.

Chapter 14

It was early spring 1942, Japan had attacked America. The Royal Navy had lost *Prince of Wales* and *Repulse* off Singapore, along with *Hermes*, two heavy cruisers and numerous destroyers and escorts, on another of Churchill's foolish errands.

Preston had finished her workup in Scapa Flow and was awaiting her next assignment — to escort a convoy to Murmansk.

Lee was sat in his day cabin, the Pilot, Watson, had been appointed his No. 1, Alf Matley had been promoted to Commander and had taken command of a new 'Hunt' class destroyer, *Melbreak*. Chief Jones was still in charge of the engines (he should have transferred to a shore job, but refused, to stay on *Preston*). Beddall had been transferred to *Viscount* as second-in-command, his replacement was a very shallow man called Ives. The navigator was a RNVR sailor from *King Alfred* called Backhouse. Watson said he would keep his eye on him. There were also four new midshipmen. Fortunately, he had managed to retain the Coxswain and Buffer, and a new doctor, Jeffries. But also lost another 100 seasoned sailors. The replacements were even younger than the last draft!

"It looks like a trip up to Murmansk," said Lee, over a cup of tea, "Make sure you check that all these new baby sailors have got cold weather clothing, the Artic in March was not a good place to be."

A knock on the door, "Signal, sir." came the shout from the Royal Marine sentry.

"Very good."

"So, I have to report to the flagship at 1300, make the launch ready No. 1."

As he crossed Scapa Flow, the launch was battered by sleet and rain and a nasty chop had started, making the crossing uncomfortable. Soon they were alongside *HMS Iron Duke*. She had taken on the role of Fleet Flagship. Being Jellicoe's flagship in WWI, she had been retained as a training ship between the wars. But on transfer to the Orkneys, she had been bombed by the Germans and had to be beached to save her from sinking. She had been disguised as to look like she was still in commission, so managed to fulfil a useful war function. The usual pipe as he stepped on the quarterdeck, and Lee turned to salute the ships flag. The harassed Flag Lieutenant, stepped forward to greet him. Why do all Flag Lieutenants look harassed, thought Lee. Ushered below out of the wind and rain, Lee stepped into the relative calm of Jellicoe's old cabin.

The Admiral stood to greet him, "Hello Alan, nice to see you again, I notice you were incorrectly dressed?"

Looking down at himself, Lee could not find anything amiss with his uniform, so asked, "Sir, I don't understand?"

The Admiral laughs, "You should have four rings up instead of three, congratulations CAPTAIN Lee!" Lee was shocked, he had no idea. After a few pleasantries and a celebratory drink, they sat down to discuss his orders.

"OK, the Russians are getting stroppy about the deliveries of cargo. As you know, we have been struggling to supply their demands. The Fleet has suffered badly over the past two years, but new ships were coming on line in increasing numbers, so we might see some results later this year. The last convoy was a disaster, 50% of the ships did not make it, and Uncle Joe has been bending Churchill's ear about it, so we were sending a large convoy next week, with as many escorts as we could manage. We have had to strip the Atlantic and Home Fleet for sufficient escort ships.

"Now you have reached the dizzy heights of Captain, you will take temporary charge of the Close Cruiser Covering Force, your call sign will be Force X. This will consist of three cruisers and four destroyers. Your orders are to cover the outbound convoy to Murmansk and Archangel, and bring back a convoy of empties that have been sat there for months, we need those ships."

"The Home Fleet will also sail, and be very distant cover near Bear Island, if you should need them.

Intelligence reports that *Tirpitz* and others may sail to intercept the outbound convoy. Questions?"

They discussed routing, fuel, logistics, and orders for the next two hours, then Lee was dismissed and he returned to his ship. As the launch reached the gangway, Lee was surprised to see a full side party, Royal Marine Guard of Honour, and seamen drawn up in divisions. On reaching the quarterdeck he was met by No 1. and all the officers, and cheering from his men, he was shocked — what the...? Then Timmins stepped forward with his uniform jacket with four gold rings on the sleeves. Someone had told them about his promotion. What a nice gesture.

The cruiser force would comprise of his cruiser *Preston*, her sistership *Manchester*, and the eight-inch gun cruiser, *Suffolk*, with the destroyers *Offa*, *Opportune*, *Onslow* and *Oribi*. The Captains were called onboard for a conference. *Manchester* and *Offa* were missing, they would join in Iceland. Once they had left his ship, he made his way to see the Captain of the Convoy Escort Group, onboard *Duncan*, where he had a talk about tactics. After a long day he returned to his ship, were he was met and invited to the wardroom to celebrate his promotion. A long night ahead.

Tuesday the following week saw the group head out of Scapa, out through the Stromness Boom, making for Iceland and the first part of the journey began. The ships pitched and rolled, it was very uncomfortable in a beam sea. All was quite as them made progress. Destiny awaited. Watson, who had taken over from Matley, as the ships Executive Officer, had ordered regular exercises for the ship's company, he wanted them sharp for what was ahead.

A few days later, they entered the Fleet anchorage at Akureyri in Iceland. Here *Manchester* and *Offa* were waiting. First line of business, make sure everybody had filled up to the brim with fuel. Last minute orders had come aboard. They sailed the following morning, this great armada.

The convoy formed up and started their plod towards Russia. Force X (Lee's group), followed later in the day, their job was not to stay close to the Cargo ships, but to be about twenty-five to fifty miles away between the convoy and Norway, as a shield. Lee ordered the ships into line abreast with *Manchester* to port and *Suffolk* to starboard, and of course *Preston* in the middle. The destroyers about ten miles ahead, were also in line abreast. Lee wanted to remain in radar contact with the convoy, so kept within fifty miles of it. The sea was dark and sullen, with occasional snow flurries, visibility was very limited, he could just make out the outline of the nearest Destroyer *Offa*.

The following morning, there was thick sea fog, visibility was very bad, so all the ships streamed fog buoys, and showed blue stern lamps. On the bridge radar repeater, Lee watched his Force as they crawled forward, relying on the invisible eye of radar. Occasional signals arrived from the Admiralty regarding the convoy. At midnight, Lee was awoken by the Chief Yeoman. "Top secret for you sir."

"Thanks, Chief. Rouse the Cipher Officer, and have it decoded, thanks."

Awake and dressed, Lee made his way to the bridge, where Timmins was awaiting with a mug of sweet strong Ky, bless him. A few moments later, Lt John Jones the Cipher Officer appeared with the signal. "Indications show, *Hipper*, *Lutzow* and *Seydlitz* and destroyers have steam up and preparing to sortie later today from Altafjord, in Norway take all necessary action to protect the convoy." Lee retired to the chart room to study the charts. After a while he called Watson and Backhouse to the chart room to join him. A plan of action was decided upon. If the enemy came straight out and direct towards them, they would be here by nightfall tomorrow. So, they would have to be ready.

The disposition of the force was altered slightly with, the destroyers deployed more north easterly than before. As if on cue the sea started to rise and the barometer began to drop, they were in for another storm.

The following day, they were spotted by a German maritime patrol aircraft, the Bv. 138, 'The Flying Clog'. Out of gun range, it circled for a while, then headed off to the west in search of the convoy. Lee kept his Force between Norway and the convoy at about forty miles range. The seas got steeper, and the temperature dropped to well below freezing, the likelihood of rescue in these temperatures were very slim. Lee shivered at the thought of that. At midday they got the signal they had been dreading, the Germans had sailed. Followed two hours later, by another signal from a friendly Sunderland flying boat, the Germans had been spotted heading north west at 20 knots, range 150 miles away.

On contact with *Duncan*, her Captain suggested that he turned the convoy round for twelve hours, to throw the Germans of the scent, then resume his course for Russia. Lee agreed, he would go in search of the German force. Force X increased speed, the sea has now risen to storm force, with seas thirty-foot-high. The destroyers were making heavy weather of it, so they had to slow down, Lee did not want to lose contact with the destroyers. Then *Offa* reported two men overboard, and turned back to look for them. He knew it was a hopeless task, but had to try anyway. Lee told him to look for one hour then re-join the force. Night had fallen, when they received another signal from the Sunderland, which now reported the Germans 75 miles away and closing on his position. Force X had to slow down again, they were struggling in this weather. The destroyers were rolling badly, but he realistically couldn't send them away, he was already outnumbered and out-gunned, so needed them. *Offa* had still not returned and had failed to answer on the TBS system. Yet they still ploughed on, what seemed like a lifetime later the first echo appeared on the radar repeater, at maximum range. Lee ordered the ship's company to have evening meal, and they change into clean clothing, then Action Stations were called.

He orders the Cruisers to change formation, with *Manchester* leading the line, then *Preston* and finally *Suffolk*. The destroyers were ordered to the portside and in line astern. They were to attack at the best opportunity. The range kept dropping, it was now thirty miles, the enemy ships remained in cruising formation, they knew force X was near. It was a filthy night, pitch black and the temperature was showing minus five degrees. The gun crews were trying hard to keep the ice build-up on their weapons to a minimum. Still they closed, the enemy had not changed formations yet, they were still unaware of Force Xs position.

At 18,000 yards Lee turned to Starboard, ordered *Suffolk* to illuminate the Germans by starshell, and *Preston*, *Manchester* and *Suffolk* to open fire using radar ranging. This the new black box fitted during the refit, and now to be used in anger for the first time.

The five German destroyers were struggling in the seaway, they were very poor seaboats, being bow heavy, and with little reserve buoyancy, they took the waves clear over their bridges, submerging them completely, making it a miserable existence for the crews. *Hipper*, *Lutzow* and *Seydlitz* were still lined abreast, with the destroyers in front, they were groping about in the dark for the convoy.

It was a classic case of crossing the enemy's T, Force X was in the perfect position to hit the enemy hard. *Suffolk's* starshells exploded above the enemy ships, illuminating them in a deathly glow, followed immediately by salvos from Force X. There was chaos onboard the enemy vessels. *Manchester* straddled *Hipper*, one hit on her stern. *Preston* also straddles *Seydlitz*, while *Suffolk* first salvo fell short of *Lutzow*. Even with the new gunnery 'Black box', in these atrocious seas, it was difficult to get a hit on the German ships. The firing continued for five minutes before the enemy started to retaliate. After twenty minutes, Force X finally gained some hits on the enemy. *Seydlitz* was hit repeatedly by *Preston* and hauled out of line on fire. *Manchester* had now been exchanging shots with *Hipper*, but then *Hipper's* fire slackened, so *Manchester* must have been doing something right. But poor *Suffolk* was taking a pounding from *Lutzow*, whose eleven-inch shells were tearing *Suffolk* apart. *Preston* changed target, and commenced firing on *Lutzow*. Salvo after salvo tore though the night sky, *Lutzow* was hit and straddled. Finally the German destroyers managed to get between the disappearing enemy cruisers and lay down a smoke screen. Lee was fearful of a torpedo attack, so hauled off to starboard, to try to work around the screen. *Manchester* followed, but poor *Suffolk*, had to reduce speed. *Opportune*, *Onslow* and *Oribi*, had finally caught up, and went tearing though the smoke screen to attack the enemy.

Onboard *Suffolk* they watched as *Preston* and *Manchester* disappeared into the night, their gunfire lighting up the darkness. *Suffolk* had been hit badly in a boiler and engine room, so her speed had dropped, and 'X' turret was out of action. The crew started to do what repairs they could. A short time later a ship appeared out of the night and started to flash VVV. This meant nothing to *Suffolk*, but they quickly realised that it was a German Maass class destroyer, who was closing in on them. The DCT started to track the enemy, when in an opportune position *Suffolk* unleashed hell on the destroyer, within seconds it was a flaming wreck, as her forward turrets exploded skywards and the bridge structure collapsed into a mangled mess. Within five minutes, it had turned turtle and sunk, there were no survivors.

Preston and *Manchester*, had skirted round the smoke and were chasing the Germans, but running with a following sea, they couldn't catch up, firing with the aid of radar, they were soon out of range. Lee had no option but to return to act as a screen for the convoy. They collected *Suffolk* on the way back to the convoy. Because of her damage *Suffolk* was ordered to place herself in the centre of the convoy, and proceed to Russia. The destroyers returned, having been unable to engage the German heavy ships, but they did have a running fight with the enemy destroyers. They reported that they did manage to torpedo a destroyer, but couldn't confirm it. *Offa* never re-joined the convoy, she was caught by the retreating Germans, who pounded her mercilessly until she sank. Again there were no survivors. The convoy continued on.

At daybreak, the 'Flying Clog' was back, circling just out of gun range. The first air raid started an hour later, Ju 88 bombers and He111 torpedo bombers. The gun crews soon got into the rhythm. After this derisory attack, they headed home, no damage to Force X reported. Thirty minutes after the attack, another force of bombers approached, but they avoided Force X and headed for the convoy. This formed the rest of the daylight hours, roughly every thirty minutes bombers making for the convoy, with an occasional attack on Lee's ships. At the end of a grim day, the radio and TBS told the story of the ships hit and sunk. Lee decided to close the convoy and offered the cargo ships the protection of his Force's anti-aircraft guns. It was a gamble, because if the German surface forces came back, he would be in a poor tactical position.

For two long days the ships were harried by German aircraft. Force Xs guns appeared to make a difference and a few bombers didn't return to their base in Norway. With no further losses amongst the convoy, they continued to Murmansk. As they crossed the top of Norway and entered the Arctic, the sea temperature dropped like a stone, the storm had abated, but the sea was full of menace. Still the attacks came. Its 1300 hours, *Preston's* crew were exhausted, and a lull in the air raids was welcomed. A terrific explosion occurred on the far side of the convoy. *Mary Elizabeth*, an

American ammunition ship, disintegrated after a torpedo attack from a submerged U-boat. The escorts on that side, chased around dropping depth charges. There was nothing to show for the effort, the U-boat had slunk away.

"Radar... Bridge, we have five surface echoes approaching from the east, sir."

"Very good, that will be the addition escort ships," said Lee.

The additional escorts bore down on the convoy, two British minesweepers and three Russian destroyers. The escort commander on *Duncan*, asked the minesweepers to sweep them into Murmansk. The Russian ships ignored all signals, cruised around the convoy, then reported they were short of fuel, and headed back to harbour. As you can imagine, the comments from 'Jack' weren't complimentary. Overhead, two Hurricane fighters of the RAF arrived overhead for protection. The ships for Archangel broke off with a small number of the escort and headed for the Kara Sea.

As they entered the Murmansk anchorage, the next air raid started, all close-range weapons commenced firing. The escort force headed for the oiler, they didn't want to hang around for longer than necessary.

Suffolk was berthed next to the coaling wharf, she was trying to effect repairs herself, they all knew there would be little help from their Russian allies. *Preston* berthed outboard of *Suffolk*. Lee had to call on the

British O.I.C. He crossed *Suffolk* and went down her gangway to the jetty. There he was met by a brutal-looking Russian soldier, who stopped him getting off the ship. A confrontation occurred, where the soldier threatened Lee with his bayonet and attempted to push him back onboard. This brought a howl of anger from *Suffolk's* crew, who started to come down the gangway en-mass. Just then a Jeep skidded to a halt next to the soldier, and Royal and Russian Navy officers got out. Without waiting for an explanation, the Russian Officer started to beat the soldier about the head with his pistol. This brought another growl from the ship's company.

"Hello Captain Lee, I am Cummins, welcome to Russia, this was Yuri Belenko, Captain Red Banner Fleet Northern Waters." Lee shook hands, he could see the spittle on the face of Belenko, and the anger in his eyes from the soldier's confrontation.

"I am sorry Captain; these soldiers were uncouth peasants," Belenko spoke in perfect English, "Please come this way," and he returned to the Jeep and jumped in the back.

Cummins weaved his way round the docks towards the Royal Navy Officer-In-Command's building. He was struck by the complete desolation of the place, it was a shambles. An ancient shunting engine was struggling to drag some trucks through the snow, its drive wheels skidding on the icy rails. Bomb craters were commonplace, unless they were blocking something of importance, they were left unfilled.

Packing crates left standing in deep pools of water, ammunition and aircraft engines left in the open, snow and ice covering everything. The stevedores shuffled around in drab grey clothing, looking at the ground, they never looked up as they passed. They continued past a line of brand-new tanks and trucks. Halfway down it, there were two men with paint and brushes, watched by a NKVD sentry, and their job was to paint out any reference to the USA or the UK. Nobody was to know these were gifts from the Allies. Cummins looked at Alan's face, and saw the look of anger on it. He caught his eye, and shook his head, not now, was the warning. They pulled up outside a dank, dark, concrete building, the only sign of colour was the Naval ensign at the entrance. Again, two surly-looking NKVD guards check there I.D. They were then allowed to enter the building. It was as cold as the outside, greatcoats and gloves, were the order of the day. Here Belenko left them alone.

Alan was introduced to the Royal Navy Officer-in-Command, Jerome, by name, who was responsible for liaising with the Russian Navy, "Hello Captain, nice to see a fresh face."

Lee saluted and shook his hand. "I need you to take onboard 171 seamen, survivors of sunken RN ships, and take them home, if they stay here, they will starve to death. The damn Russians won't let us use the supplies that have been brought here for our own use, they claim they are damaged and we can't access them, poppycock!" There is a hospital of sorts, people go in, but never come out, take these lads home, they deserve better." Jerome was clearly distressed by the treatment of the sailors, ships, and cargo by our glorious ally.

"All they ever complain about is that this or that has not arrived, they have no idea what the crews are going through to get the cargo here. Those destroyers you saw, never left the quay, and when they do, they come back literally straight away. When the Italians sold the Russians that design, they knew they were too lightly built for the Arctic, so they don't and can't go far from port. It's disgraceful.

"Alan, please tell the Admiralty what is going on here, the Russians heavily censor my messages, so I don't think they get through to London. They won't let the crews get off the ships, they don't supply victuals for the return trips, and they charge us for the fuel, it's our fuel we brought for them!"

Clearly the pressure was getting to Jerome, but Lee promised to do all he could, when he returned to the ship. The least he could do, was to make sure supplies were landed for the RNOIC. But even this was intercepted by the NVKD Russian security police, who took half of it for themselves.

Later, a long line of bedraggled sailors shuffled down the quay, escorted by armed guards, like convicts, they were dressed only with the clothes they were wearing when the ship was lost, the Russians wouldn't give them a change of clothes. Corpses were robbed of clothing to help out. Lee was furious at their treatment. But there was little he could do, as soon as they were onboard, they were taken down to the mess decks, given hot showers, fresh clothes and a hot meal. Every single matelot thanked Lee for his help.

The next day, they cast off and proceeded down the estuary. *Manchester* fell in astern; the escorts moved out to do an anti-U-boat sweep ahead of the cruisers. *Suffolk* had not finished repairs, so had to be left behind. It was a bitter blow to her crew, they did not want to remain here, but without repairs she would not be able to keep up with the cruiser force. The empty convoy of cargo ships had left earlier, and Force X passed them to take up their screening role. The sea was rough and the cargo ships wallowed and staggered as the wind and wave action hit them, as they left the shelter of the land. They headed north and then north west hoping to escape the attention of the Luftwaffe. Once again, the weather was against them as another storm tore down on them. The sky turned black, and the wind rose to storm force. The ships soon become scattered as each master tried to protect his ship from the violence of the elements. After twenty-four hours of this, it was every ship for themselves, even the cruisers were heave to, head to wind, to try to save the ship. Safety lines were rigged and all movement on the upper deck was barred. Yet again ready-use lockers, life rafts, spars, guardrails were all torn off and disappeared into the monstrous seas. The lower yard arm sixty feet above the waterline, disappeared, along with the radio aerials. The surface search radar had been knocked of its turntable and leant drunkenly to one side.

The other escorts were also taking it poorly, many reporting major damage and leaks. Yet still the winds howled like banshees. *Onslow* was suffering; the main deck had split and had created a major leak. Lee ordered her to follow *Manchester*, who was pumping oil overboard to create a more moderate seas to help *Onslow* effect repairs. This action helped a little.

For two long days the storm roared on, then it started to abate. With no surface radar, *Preston* was blind, so had to rely on *Manchester* for the position of the convoy. The convoy escort were desperately trying to round up the stragglers, but many of the ships had vanished, either by enemy action, self-preservation, or the force of the seas. Of thirty-eight ships that left Russia, twenty-one were still in contact, also two corvettes and a rescue trawler were missing.

As dawn broke the following day, the sea had calmed, and visibility had improved, but the temperature had again, dropped well below zero. With the sun came the recon aircraft, staying well out of gun range. All the ships braced themselves for what was surely to come. Also, on the horizon, belching clouds of black smoke, came the rescue trawler *Fleetwood Maid*, along with four of the missing merchant ships. Two destroyers were sent back to give them some protection. By mid-day the convoy was reunited and they continued to the west, and safety. The Boatswain and a dozen men were going around the ship assessing the damage and trying to do some repairs. Lee watched them as they struggled on the icy deck. The superstructure was starting to get an accumulation of ice, so Watson had ordered a working party to try and reduce the top weight. The air search radar and the lookouts scanned the skies.

Timmins arrived on the bridge, with a cup of coffee and a cheese sandwich. Turning to thank him, Lee noticed a flash of light over near the convoy, followed a few seconds later by a dull explosion. Another explosion followed, the destroyer, *Achates,* and *Empire Shell*, an empty oil tanker, had been torpedoed. In a well-planned manoeuvre the escorts on that side of the convoy turned to hunt down the U-Boat as *Fleetwood Maid* headed for the tanker and the corvette, *Snowdrop*, dropped back to help *Achates*.

The tanker was soon underway again, the damage was confined to an empty oil tank, which was sealed off and the ship had resumed its position in the convoy. Poor *Achates* was doomed, the torpedo had destroyed the bulkhead between the engine and boiler rooms and she was slowly sinking by the bow. *Snowdrop* took off the crew, and the confidential books were thrown overboard in a weighted bag. She then dropped a depth charge alongside *Achates* to speed up the sinking. This was not a place to be hanging around. *Achate*'s stern rose high into the sky and she slipped quickly into the deep, a moment later a huge water spout rose from the sea, her depth charges had exploded, somebody forgot to set them to safe. *Snowdrop* re-joined the convoy, her crew increased two-fold with the survivors onboard. Of the submarine, there was no sign.

Just before sunset, the Luftwaffe arrived, again a mixed formation of He111 torpedo bombers and Ju 88 dive bombers. The escorts open fire, the usual cacophony assaulted the ears. Three He 111 got shot down and a Junkers, and only one bomb hit on the unlucky *Empire Shell*, which again was able to continue. The sea had remained calm, as if mocking the efforts of men. The ship had to endure another bitterly cold night. Watson took a turn around the deck to check on everything. He came across a sailor at his post in a 20mm gun tub, on approach Watson did not get a reply to his greeting. Annoyed, he shouted at the sailor, no response — asleep on duty — not on my watch. He grabbed the man, who slumped over the breach block of his gun, dead! Apparently, he had been leaning on the gun tub heater, which had failed in the intense cold, the man had not noticed and had slipped into a hypothermic sleep, and passed away. Yet another casualty of the insanity of this war.

When they returned to Iceland again, they were all dispersed to their different destinations, mostly by joining other convoys. *Preston, Manchester* and the three destroyers made their way to Scapa, from there *Preston* headed for Cammell Lairds in Birkenhead for repairs to the storm damage, and leave was given for seven days for each watch.

Lee was summoned down to the Admiralty in London, where he met the First Sea Lord, Dudley Pound, and was asked to elaborate on the report he forwarded about the convoy. After the meeting, Mr. AV Alexander, The First Lord of the Admiralty, joined them, who also wanted a briefing. After this he led down to the Map Room, where he found out what was going on with the war. Admiral Pound then told Lee, he was to take *Preston* to Gibraltar, where they were to escort a major convoy to Malta. This would be called Operation Pedestal. After the operation was over Lee would leave *Preston* and assume command of a new aircraft carrier.

Chapter 15

Re-joining the ship at Birkenhead, he was pleased to see the repairs were well underway. Around the Mersey he noticed lots of new warships going about their business. Finally, the building program was starting to show results. Across from *Preston's* berth, at Cammell Lairds, Lee could see his new command taking shape on the building slip — the aircraft carrier, *Invincible*.

Yet again, seasoned sailors had left the ship, and a new draft of HO sailors had arrived. Watson looked down on them from the bridge, "Here we go again!" he muttered.

A familiar face appeared at the gangway asking for permission to come aboard, Alf Matley, ex No. 1, now promoted to Captain of his own ship, the *Melbreak*. Being an accomplished painter, he had done a rendition of *Preston* at speed, and was presenting it to the ship, to be hung in the wardroom.

Later in the wardroom, the familiar fug of pipe and cigarette smoke assaulted Lee as he entered the room to meet his friend, as a non-smoker he finds the smell distasteful, but accepted that some men needed the nicotine fix! A couple of his officers were a little worse for the drink and were making a noise in the area near the piano. They sat in a corner with Watson and had a pleasant discussion on the way the war was being conducted. All too soon the gathering broke up. Matley had to re-join his ship, and left on the next tide, bound for the Plymouth command.

Soon, *Preston's* repairs were completed, and she sailed for Liverpool Bay to conduct trials and adjustments, and he was satisfied with the ship, he signalled the Admiralty that he was ready for sea.

New orders were received. He was to proceed to the 'Tail o' the Bank' at Greenock and report to Rear Admiral Burrough onboard the *Nigeria*. Leaving the next morning, it's a beautiful warm summer's day, the sea was calm and the visibility unlimited. The radar continued its unceasing vigil, the lookouts searched their appointed sectors. The defence watch was in place, and he could hear the scrape of ammunition belts on the side of the gun positions as the ship rolled. Timmins had brought a cup of coffee to the bridge. After the hell of the Arctic, this was a very pleasant occasion and he intended to enjoy the warmth and serenity. In the distance he could see a couple of corvettes conducting an anti-submarine sweep and a Sunderland flying boat was circling the scene. The bridge watch went about their business, and a quiet discussion was going on in the far corner of the bridge about the merits of horseracing!

As they closed the corvettes, one flashed a signal. "From *Fennel* sir, nice to see you again," reported the Chief Yeoman.

Lee smiled, "Make to *Fennel* from *Preston*, thank you for the protection last time, stay safe, see you again."

They continued northwards to Glasgow. A few hours later, the Chief Yeoman arrived on the bridge, "Sir we have intercepted a signal from *Wallflower*, it reads, '*Fennel* lost with all hands after striking a mine!'"

"Bloody Hell Chief, will it ever end!" Lee left the bridge with the signal in his hand and made his way to his sea cabin, he needed to be alone.

It was a very sombre ship's company that anchored off Greenock the following day. "Signal sir, Captain to repair onboard at 1000 hours tomorrow." Lee looked around the anchorage, and saw *Manchester* and *Cairo* also here. Two old 'chummy ships'. "Bunts, ask *Manchester* and *Cairo* to come aboard for drinks at 1900 tonight. Ships company four hours leave, 1800, No. 1." Might as well have some relaxation, thought Lee.

"Aye, sir, duty oiler will be here at 1500."

"Thanks, No. 1."

At 1000 next day, Lee was standing on the quarterdeck of *Nigeria*, along with a throng of other Captains, soon they were all ushered down to the wardroom, which had been cleared to get so many people in one place. An armed Marine stood guard on the wardroom door, and all identities were checked, and the pantry hatch had been closed and latched.

Admiral Burrough began speaking, "Gentlemen, thanks for joining us, smoke if you wish, no notes were to be taken at this moment, all the details would be in your sealed orders when you get them. I would broadly spell out what we were doing.

"We will be embarking on the largest convoy to go to Malta to date. With the halting of convoys to Russia, we now have sufficient ships to escort this convoy through. It will comprise of two battleships, four aircraft carriers, nine cruisers, thirty-five destroyers, six corvettes, four mine sweepers, nine submarines, two rescue tugs and three fleet oilers. We will be there, to protect fourteen merchantmen, which includes one fast tanker. Whatever the cost these merchant ships MUST GET THROUGH. Again, whatever the cost! The Fleet in Alexandria will also sail in support, and if needed, act as a decoy."

A whistle went around the room and a gentle murmur started.

"OK settle down, the bulk of the Fleet will escort the convoy until it reaches the Skerki Bank area, then it will withdraw. The carriers will fly off a deck load of Spitfires, which will head for Malta, be rearmed and refueled, then return to give protection over the convoy. *Preston*, *Manchester*, *Nigeria*, *Kenya* and *Cairo* will continue with the convoy and its escort to give protection until they arrive at Malta. The fleet oilers and their escorts will turn back before Skerki, so make sure your ships were topped up with fuel before they leave.

The subs will be stationed in a line between ourselves and the Eyeties, and should be well north of us.

"You will receive your orders soon, and we all have different departure times and instructions on what was needed, but we will be passing Gibraltar on the night of 9/10 August no matter what.

"Now these orders are Top Secret, tell your Number Ones and the Navigators, but no-one else. Understood?" Nods all round. "Right, the sun is over the yardarm? Drinks all round?"

Later, Lee descended the ladder and settled onto the stern seat in *Preston's* launch, "Back to the ship sir?" Lee nodded. "Off to Malta again, are we, sir?" the coxswain asked. Lee smiled, so much for security!

The next few days were a hive of activity, extra rations, survival gear and ammunition was brought onboard.

Preston sailed with *Cairo* and three destroyers, first to the Irish Sea to conduct manoeuvres and to exercise the ship's crew. Then onward to Gibraltar, the plan was for this formation to enter the harbour, refuel and leave again as soon as possible, heading back into the Atlantic and await out of sight of land, join up with the convoy, and re-enter the Mediterranean after dark, to avoid unwanted eyes spotting them. All went well with the refuelling, but the convoy was spotted passing back though the Straits, in the dead of night, by a Spanish fishing boat. The radio message back to Berlin read,

"Large number of ships heading east." The secret was out.

The convoy forms up, at 15 knots this was a very fast convoy. These were all modern, fast merchant ships. With a line of destroyers out front, five cruisers in line abreast behind the destroyers, with *Preston* the extreme left-hand ship, following the destroyers, and a compact box of merchantmen, surrounded by other escort ships and the three anti-aircraft cruisers, bringing up the rear, the battleships and carriers. Overhead a flight of Sea Hurricane fighters circled the convoy ready to pounce on any enemy.

Lee looked around at the fleet as it proceeded towards its destination. Watson was with him. "I have never seen so many warships in one place! It looks like a fleet regatta." They both laughed. Being the far-left hand ship, *Preston* was very aware that she would be closest to the enemy when they attacked. The radar scanned the horizon, and extra lookouts had been posted. Extra vigilance would be needed. Watson turned to Lee, "It's nice to feel warm again, after the Arctic." A shiver ran down his spine.

"Yes, No. 1, it is, and if anything happens, we will have a better chance of survival in the warm sea." Night fell on the first day, all was quiet. The ship settled down for the night. Lee was uncomfortable, he had a feeling that something was wrong.

The next day, dawned, warm and sunny with unlimited visibility, and a gentle swell.

"Radar... Bridge, single aircraft due south heading north, if it stays on course will pass straight over us."

Action Stations, again the alarm rattlers sounded. Three fighters went snarling over the convoy, heading south to intercept the intruder. A short time later, the TBS squawked, "Ignore, the aircraft is Vichy French, heading for mainland France."

"Bugger, there goes our position, the enemy will know where we were now!" hissed Lee.

At 1145 *Furious* started launching her cargo of Spitfires for the 580-mile trip to Malta. Fifteen mins later there was a dull boom felt and heard on the bridge. All eyes turned in the direction of the sound. At the rear of the convoy a large cloud of black smoke could be seen. "Bridge... DCT, what can you see?" Being higher up, they have a better view.

Again, the TBS squawks, "*Eagle* has been torpedoed, *Lookout* to standby for survivors, everybody else stay on course."

Eight mins later the aircraft carrier *Eagle* had sunk, and with her went one third of the fighters needed for the defence of the convoy. The submarine, U-73 slunk away, avoiding retribution. Lee looked around the bridge, some of the new hands looked aghast, but he knew more was to come. One bright spot, after *Furious* had launched all her Spitfires and turned for home. One of her escorting destroyers, *Wolverine*, ran down and sank the Italian submarine *Dogabur*.

Just as the sun was setting thirty Italian aircraft attacked from the north east. The Fleet closed ranks and engaged the aircraft, with no losses or damage, the enemy lost three aircraft, these falling to the guns of the escorting fighters. Another restless night, as the ship's crew awaited developments.

Again, the dawn broke to a warm, cloudless sky. The crew moved around the ship doing essential jobs. Watson was the Officer of the watch; he also had a strange feeling. He spoke, "Snotty," (the universal name for midshipmen) "Take the Bo'sun with you and check the emergency equipment in all the rafts and boats, and make good any discrepancies."

Mr Vickers replied, "Yes, sir." and scampered off.

"Mr Sidwell," the other midshipman, "go around the ship, and make sure everyone is wearing life jackets, take the Cox'n with you." He also rushed off.

At ten o'clock a raid of 10 JU88 aircraft caused no damage and scurried off home, chased by three fighters.

Just as the hands were being called for lunch, the tannoy announced, "Action Stations, one hundred plus aircraft from the north." Mess trays and benches were sent flying as the crew rush to their action stations. Overhead nine fighters were clawing for altitude to break up this attack. On the bridge Lee watched in fascination as these bombers, who were definitely the 'A' Team, went about their deadly business with gusto. Twisting and turning, the ships took measures to avoid the deadly bombs. Lee had to admit these SM79s was better than he faced last year. At 1330 the lead ship of the port column, *Deucalion*, the nearest merchant ship to *Preston,* was hit by a string of bombs. She slowed down and pulled out of line, she was down by the bow, and the destroyer, *Bramham* was ordered to escort her south and to make their own way to Malta. *Victorious* was hit on the flight deck, but fortunately it failed to explode.

Silence settled over the convoy. A time to recover, restock ammunition bins and take a hasty meal.

As they approached the Skerki Bank, the ships of the covering force, turned back, and the convoy had to change formation into a long two ship column, with *Preston* leading the port column. A massed air raid began, with squadron after squadron of enemy aircraft attacking the ships. Luftwaffe JU87s, singled out the carrier *Indomitable*, and hit her with three large bombs, causing huge fires and devastation onboard. *Foresight* was hit by two bombs, and rolled over and sank. There was a slight pause, then as night fell, a coordinated attack by aircraft, Italian submarines, MAS (Italian torpedo boats) and E-Boats, was made on the convoy.

On the bridge Lee was trying to make sense of it all. His AA battery was in constant use, the sound of spent brass cases, clanging onto the deck, the lines of tracer bullets criss-crossed the sky, along with the general cacophony of noise was unbelievable. All around him, *Nigeria* was hit by two torpedoes, and had stopped, *Ohio*, the Tanker, was hit by a torpedo, *Cairo* was hit by torpedoes and sank, *Kenya* was hit and stopped, *Clan Ferguson* was sunk, *Brisbane Star*, damaged, and *Empire Hope* sunk. Still, they moved on, on, ever on they went.

They approached the Cape Bon area, where the swept channel was very narrow.

"Asdic... Bridge, we can hear high speed propellers to port." E-boats!

Explosion's lightened the dark sky, *Almeria Lykes*, *Wairanga*, *Glenorchy*, *Santa Elisa*, *Wiamarama* were all sunk, *Manchester, Rochester Castle* and *Ohio*, again, all hit by MAS or E-Boat torpedoes. *Manchester* later sank in the night.

As dawn broke, they headed south east away from the coast, *Preston* was the only cruiser left. A string of damaged ships followed in their wake. Lee was bone tired, the ship was a mess, littered with shrapnel and spent ammunition cases, and weary sailors stood closed up at their positions.

"Radar... Bridge, large force of aircraft to the north forty miles." Here we go again. Luftwaffe JU 88 and JU87 bombers, Italian SM79s, wave after wave attacked the ships, his gun crews shooting like demons, more ships hit by bombs, yet they still moved forward. After a couple of hours of this they were left alone. He and his men were exhausted.

"DCT... Bridge, Captain we were running very short of AA ammunition."

"Thanks, Guns."

"Man overboard, starboard side," came the shout. Lee's heart sank, he could not turn back.

"Signal *Penn* to search for him." Ives came running onto the bridge, tears streaming down his cheeks. "Sir, it was L.S. Burns, we had just finished firing, when he took off his harness, and his lifejacket, and said, 'Sorry lads, I have to go' and jumped overboard." The seaman had been onboard since commissioning and had clearly reached the end of his tether.

"OOW make an entry in the log, LS Burns, discharged dead." At least his family would know he died a hero.

A few moments later, the ship shuddered as if shaken by a strong hand, there was a tremendous explosion forward, and the entire 'A' gun and the forecastle disappeared, the barrels of 'B' turret were folded back like pieces of straw, the turret jammed. Damage control parties rushed forward to deal with the damage. Chief Jones, came up to the bridge and before he could speak, there was another explosion, followed by a third, in quick succession. *Preston* had entered an unknown minefield, laid by the Italians the night before. A fourth explosion at the stern, and the ship was doomed. She was settling lower in the water, and starting to list to port.

"CPO send a signal to the Admiralty, copy Force 'H', and Admiral Burrough, tell them we are sinking, due to mine damage, get our position off the Pilot, send plain language. Mr Vickers, make sure the confidential books are thrown overboard. No. 1, go round the ship and get everybody out and into the boats and rafts."

"Bunts, ask that destroyer," Lee pointed over the side, "*Wilton*, to rescue survivors."

Abandon ship.

Glossary

40mm/Bofors: A Swedish anti-aircraft weapon

ABC: Admiral of the Fleet, Andrew Browne Cunningham

Adrift: Late/absent from place of duty

ANZAC: Acronym for Australian and New Zealand troops

Ashore: Going outside the establishment you're living in

Bimble: Walk

Blockade runner: Enemy merchant ship that is trying to run the blockade back to a home port

Brass hat: Any officer with gold braid on the peak of his cap

Bulkhead: Wall

Bunts: Slang for signalman or bunting tossers

Call the hands: Get out of bed

Civvies: Civilian clothing

Chum: Mate

Chummy ship: Ships that work together

Class leader: A selected member of your class

Clean ship/cleaning stations: Sweeping/mopping/scrubbing—prepare for rounds

Clubswinger/clubs: Physical training instructor

CPO/Chief petty officer: Addressed as 'Chief'
Chief yeoman: CPO in charge of the signal department
Daily dits: Daily orders
DCT: Director control tower, from where they target the guns
Deck: Floor
Deckhead: Ceiling
Defaulters' table: where the punishment is awarded for poor behaviour
Dhobi dust: Washing powder
Dhobying: Washing (clothes), usually by hand
Dit: A story or quote usually funny
Divisional officer: Your 'boss'
Divisions: Formal parade
Duty part of the watch: Ratings detailed for additional duties that day
Eytie: Slang for an Italian
Fly-boys: Slang for embarked aircrew.
Fall of shot: an observer spots were the shells land and redirects the aiming point for a hit
Gash: Baby or new entrant
Goffa: Drink
H.A.: High angle weapon used for firing at aircraft
Head: Toilet

Influence mine: A mine set to explode as the pressure wave of a passing ship sets of the detonation
Jabs: Vaccinations etc
Jack dustys: Supply chain logistician
Jap: Slang for a Japanese.
Jerry/Nazi/ Kraut: Slang for a German
Junior rates: Term for leading hands and below
Killick/leading hand: Addressed as Leader, Leading Hand or Hooky
Kit muster: Formal inspection of your kit
Kye: a thick gluttonous drink made from a block of chocolate and condensed milk
L.A.: For firing at enemy surface contacts and shore targets
Make-n-mend: Afternoon off
Matelot (pronounced mat-low): A sailor/naval rating
Mess/messdeck: living quarters
Muster: Collect/gather at a specific location
Nine o'clockers: Later evening meal
No 1/Jimmy: First lieutenant or executive officer
Nozzer: New entrant
Oerlikon: A Swiss made automatic 20mm anti-aircraft weapon
Oggin: The sea/water

Onboard: Inside the establishment
OOD: Officer of the day
OOW: Officer of the watch
Oppo: Close friend
Parade drill: Marching and saluting etc
Paravanes: floatation device fitted to the bow of the ship, to sweep for mines
Pipe down: Lights out, go to sleep
Pit: Bed
PO/Petty officer: Addressed as PO
Pom-pom: 2 pounder anti-aircraft weapon, gets its name from the sound it makes when firing.
Pompey: Portsmouth
Pongo: Slang for soldier,
Putty: The shore, ship on the putty, run aground
Raider: Ships like the Pocket Battleship *Graf Spee*, looking for merchant ships to sink
Rig of the day: Uniform as specified to be worn
Rounds: Formal inspection of your messdeck/toilets/bathrooms
Run ashore: Leisure time down to town
Scran: A meal
Sea dust: Salt
Secure: Stop work

Senior rates: Term for warrant officers, chiefs and petty officers

Shagbat or steam pigeon: nickname for the Supermarine Walrus Amphibian

Slide: Butter or margarine

SNAFU: Situation normal all F**ked up

Snorkers: A sausage

Stand easy: Short tea break but also a drill order

Stokers/clankies: Slang term for the men in the boiler and engine rooms

Supper: Early evening meal

TBS/Talk between ships: A first generation line of site radio telephone

Pusser/pussers: Absolutely anything issued by the Royal Navy

Turn to: Start work

Victuals: Food stuffs

WAFU: Wet and fu++ing useless

Wet: Any beverage, hot or cold

WO/Warrant officer: Addressed as 'Sir'